LIAR of KUDZU

LIAR of KUDZU

Bob Schooley
and
Mark McCorkle

Simon & Schuster Books for Young Readers
New York   London   Toronto   Sydney

SIMON & SCHUSTER BOOKS FOR YOUNG READERS
An imprint of Simon & Schuster Children's Publishing Division
1230 Avenue of the Americas, New York, New York 10020
This book is a work of fiction. Any references to historical events, real people, or
real locales are used fictitiously. Other names, characters, places, and incidents
are products of the author's imagination, and any resemblance to actual events or
locales or persons, living or dead, is entirely coincidental.
SIMON & SCHUSTER BOOKS FOR YOUNG READERS is a trademark of Simon & Schuster, Inc.
Book design by Lucy Ruth Cummins
The text for this book is set in Base 12 Serif.
Manufactured in the United States of America
10 9 8 7 6 5 4 3 2 1
Library of Congress Cataloging-in-Publication Data
Schooley, Bob.
Liar of Kudzu / Bob Schooley and Mark McCorkle.—1st ed.
p. cm.
Summary: Twelve-year-old Pete, known as Liar for his ability to stretch the truth,
teams up with the class geek and the new girl in school to investigate a strange
object from outer space.
ISBN-13: 978-1-4169-1488-4
ISBN-10: 1-4169-1488-9
[1. Honesty—Fiction. 2. Outer space—Fiction.
3. Adventure and adventurers—Fiction.] I.McCorkle, Mark. II. Title.
PZ7.S3746Lia 2006
[Fic]—dc22
2005036245

FIRST
EDITION

For our four Mommas:
Shirley
Eleanor
Alison
Stephanie
—R. S. and M. M.

ACKNOWLEDGMENTS
Thanks to Ellen Goldsmith-Vein and
Julie Kane-Ritsch for their endless enthusiasm.
And to David Gale and Alexandra Cooper
for their patient guidance.

Chapter ONE

Kudzu is the name of a nasty weed that grows like crazy down these parts. I've seen a whole house get covered over by the green vines in the space of one wet summer, until it looks like it's a habitat more suitable for hobbits than humans.

Kudzu's also the name of the town that I've lived in my whole life. I don't think the people who named the town meant for you to think it was nasty, but I think they did hope it would grow like crazy. It didn't. But that's okay. Daddy says, "More people, more problems" whenever he explains how he got a notion to move to this puny town, nearby to nowhere special.

My name is Pete Larson, but everybody calls me Liar. They don't mean no harm by it, it's just a plain fact that I am the finest truth bender in all of Dixon County. And not little weeny white lies. Big fat whopper ones that make people forget the question they asked in the first place. No shame in it. People in Kudzu appreciate a good story; it keeps things interesting.

This story I'm going to tell now, it's a good one.

It mostly happened last summer, when I just turned twelve. Dixon County schools get out in the middle of May. By then it's too hot to do many educationally worthwhile things anyway. In truth, I think by April us kids give up learning anything that'll stick. For proof you just have to look at last year's science fair. This was the big-deal final chance for extra credit, and other than Bobby Ray Dobbs—and he's a freak—nobody barely bothered. There was stuff like baking soda volcanoes, a clock made with wires stabbed into a moldy potato, and celery soaking up purple food coloring. I've seen more interesting scientific exhibits smashed dead by the side of the road. Which is why I pinned half of a skunk to poster board for my project. Probably because it was the smelly half, I think my project did more harm than good as it applied to my final grade. But at that point I didn't even care. There was just a week left and we were free. Spring fever had turned to summer fever, which is similar but with more humidity and bigger bugs.

Just when the class was fully coasting and counting the days, something highly peculiar happened: A new kid started at school. Technically it was a new girl, but the important point was that she started our homeroom with a week left to go. It was just unusual. Her name was Justine Henry and her daddy was military, which might have explained things, because people from the base seem to be particular about rules. They don't appreciate a good lie; I can tell you that from experience.

This one time I rode my bike thirteen miles over there because I'd heard they had a store that sold Hershey bars for a quarter, and I wanted to see for myself. I could see the store on the other side of the fence, and I could see ladies coming out with grocery bags heavy-full of what I figured to be twenty-five-cent candies. But no matter how many times I told the guard at the outside that my mom was in there and she had my base identification card, he would not let me past his little orange gate. And it wasn't like I wasn't convincing; I even squeezed out a single tear, which is generally a deal-closer, but not that time.

This girl, Justine, sat next to me, but that's not the reason I mention her. The reason I bring her up is because this story is about her as much as anybody else.

She smiled a little and said "I'm Justine," like she was being polite but not overly friendly or anything.

I was at a critical point, folding my last geometry test into a paper football, so I just nodded back a little and answered her with, "Liar." At this she kind of made a pinched-up face, which at first I didn't understand, until Kelly Stone behind me spoke up and said that it wasn't an insult on her but what people called me. I don't think this explanation fully satisfied her, but by that point Miss Ballast was calling roll, and I guess the damage was done.

I regretted that sour first impression, because in good truth, Justine was that rare girl who could actually be called "pretty" without attaching a "but" on the end. As in "pretty but she has horse teeth," or "pretty but dumb as a box of chalk." For one reason or another there were a lot of compromises in the looks department with the kids I'd grown up with, but Justine may have been perfect. At least that was my first impression of her.

For most of the year the walk home from school is not so bad. It might be a mile, but most of it cuts through town, and Jackson's store is at the halfway point, so there's always stopping for a Coke or comics. Then it's a long processional down Main, with the canopy elm trees shading over you. People sit in old rockers on deep front porches and follow you with their eyes as you pass, to make sure you don't do nothing funny.

But this day, with summer coming on hot, was different. The memory of that look from Justine kind of haunted me. I wished I had a time machine so I could go back and play things different. Who knew that being honest about my own name could get me into trouble that way? I decided I had four more school days to fix things between me and her, and it had better work, because otherwise she'd be back at the base all summer and by fall that first impression of old Liar would have hardened like dog poop in the sun.

Like my daddy, Momma is originally from New York City. Up there, until I was born, she was a lawyer of a type that doesn't go into courthouses or anything. Now she bakes pies, pretty good ones too. For some reason she sells them to people back in NYC for upward of thirty-five dollars—for one pie, no lie. It seems that people up east have more money for pie than some people down here have for whole suppers. Momma says that people will pay a premium for honest Southern cooking. I guess people will pay for just about anything really, if you know how to talk them into it. Momma has a website that does that job for her. Her pies look better than real on that website.

Daddy works one town over at the college. He teaches creative writing and edits a magazine called *Southern Poetry Quarterly*. I've thumbed through a few issues and noticed that the works within are suspiciously light on rhyme, not to mention reason. Once

6   *Schooley/McCorkle*

he did a whole issue on the theme of kudzu—the weed, not our town. It was no better or worse than any of the others, but it did have a pretty cool cover picture of one of them hobbit houses.

I would have liked to run over the Justine problem with either of them, but I knew from experience that this would be a mistake. Our house has a room that you could almost call a library. Two of the walls are from top to bottom bookshelves. One whole shelf is nothing but books about raising perfect children. Not that I ever met any, but I suppose these books have worked for somebody somewhere. Maybe kids in New York.

Since I'm the only minor in the house, every piece of advice in these books, most of it bad, from my view, gets tried out on me. If I should mention to Daddy that, say, I'm having nightmares—not that I do more than normal, but just for the sake of example— this is what would happen: He would stall me with dumb questions, and I'd hear Momma in the book room, frantically leafing through volume after crackpot volume, looking for just the perfect stupid solution. Sometimes I think they're a little disappointed that I came out so regular. Other than the lying, of course.

I can only imagine the fun they'd have if they could get their hands on Bobby Ray Dobbs. First of all, the kid's a science genius, and there are all kinds of programs that faculty kids can take advantage of at the college if they're motivated. Which I'm not, but Bobby Ray would be. So there's that. But even better, from the bookshelf perspective, Bobby Ray is one sick pup. His desk is stuffed with those little wetnaps in the foil packets that you can get at the Waffle House. He's constantly got his hands in there, peeling one open superslow so no one will notice. Except everyone does. Even with his wetnap routine, he still has to go to the boys' room to wash his hands about a hundred times a day. Somebody must have worked out a deal for him, because if that was me, there would be a parent conference on tap, no doubt. And the clean hands are just the beginning of the Bobby Ray weirdness list. Another thing is that he always has to walk the same certain route to his desk from the classroom

Schooley/McCorkle

door, which might not have been so noticeable if not for the hand-washing frequency. Funny thing is, you'd think a science genius would be all over that "shortest distance between two points" jazz, but for reasons that no one can figure out, Bobby Ray's classroom commute is best described as a figure 88.

Still, even though I am no Bobby Ray Dobbs, I could just picture the frenzy that would be whipped if I casually mentioned at supper that I thought the new girl was pretty. I decided to save the folks the book money by keeping it to myself.

Supper that night was another tofu dish. Momma lets me eat pretty much anything I feel like for breakfast and lunch, but she's in charge of me eating "one *good* meal" a day. As if anyone could call boiled soybean curd good, but Momma does. I figure it's the price I have to pay to be able to have Cap'n Crunch or Pop-Tarts for breakfast.

You can't really buy tofu in Kudzu, but Momma trades pies for it from somebody in California. They say tofu can taste like anything, but it's pretty poor at imitating a smoky rack of baby back ribs. Sometimes when Momma is visiting Gram Lois, Daddy will take me to Mr. Black's Rib Shack out on the highway, and we will purify ourselves of Momma's vegetarian suppers. Not that they're as wholly bad as they sound, but ribs are better. One time Momma found a wetnap from Mr. Black's in my jeans. I told her Bobby Ray gave it to me. I think she might have believed me.

It's a perplexing position, I would imagine, being the folks of a boy called Liar. Sometimes when they think I'm bluffing them, I'm seriously not. Keeps them on their toes, I suppose.

Chapter **TWO**

When I went to bed, I couldn't sleep and wasn't exactly sure why. Momma had washed my sheets that day, and usually that mountain-fresh Tide smell lulls me right off. But that night I lay wide awake and thought of a million different things. Did mountains really smell that fresh? I was pretty sure they didn't. After all, there was a lot of wildlife in the mountains, and I imagined that the bears alone . . .

Other thoughts pushed in. The night seemed to be getting hotter by the minute. Outside, the crickets and locusts were tuning up to full summer volume. It would be a feast for the nighthawks. But even they had turned in by now.

A train clanged through town. It's always kind of a

sad sound, when the whistle blows, but that night for some reason it seemed even sadder to me. When I was little, I used to pretend that it was a circus train when I'd hear that whistle and chug. I pictured it full up with pachyderms and carnivores and clowns, their heads sticking out all over like in the Little Golden Books. Really it was loaded with car parts from Japan and tanks full of chemicals that could wipe out half of Kudzu if it ever went off the rails, according to Momma, who frequently worried about things like that. On that night, the one when I couldn't sleep, I thought a lot about that train derailing and people running for their lives from a purple killer cloud. I didn't know if a chemical cloud would really be purple, but in my mind it was, and that was good enough.

When the train finally passed, and the clowns and clouds started to fade, a whip-poor-will took a shift keeping me awake. He was loud and close. His call sounded like "Don't go to SLEEP . . . Don't go to SLEEP . . . Don't go to SLEEP . . ." I knew enough about birds to know what he was really saying, though. He needed a girlfriend, and he was going to just keep yelling until he found one. I never thought I needed a girlfriend, but that night I felt like that pathetic dumb bird.

It all came down to Justine. No matter what else I tried to think about, it kept coming back to that look on her face when I'd called myself Liar. Was every night going to be like this from now on? It was crazy. If someone had told me the day before that I'd spend the night thinking about a girl, I would have said that person was nuts. But there was no getting around it now; I had to make Justine like me. Or at least not hate me.

I knew I needed to fall back on my best skills, which meant some serious truth twisting was in order. But I knew one of my spur of the moment lies wouldn't be good enough. What this called for was a plan. I was good at making plans. Usually it involved something like turning a refrigerator box into an all-terrain vehicle, so this girl thing was new territory. There were almost too many possibilities. I could do something lame like pick her a bunch of wildflowers and leave them on her desk with a note signed, "Mr. Mystery." Or I could do something lamer still, like find out her favorite singer and call his people and tell them I had some incurable kid disease but that an autographed copy of his new CD might make me miraculously better. I could find out where her family was going on vacation, and then talk my folks into going to the same place, so we'd run into each other in a strange town. I'd be a friendly face, so she'd have to talk to me and get to know the real Liar.

More plans presented themselves for my approval, and more plans didn't seem quite right. Finally, just before I dozed, I was sure I had the perfect plan, and I fell asleep happy.

Schooley/McCorkle

Chapter THREE

The next morning the whole plan, the whole bullet-proof perfect scheme, was gone.

Gone from my head like it had never even been there. All my best ideas seem to get crystal clear just before I go to sleep, and then are just vapor in the morning.

I woke up late and panicked. As I pulled on my jeans and toasted my blueberry Pop-Tart, I tried to reconstruct the plan, but it was useless. Whatever I had come up with late at night was forgotten on this muggy morning, and I had to face her, Justine, unprepared. Momma thought that my eyes had dark circles, and she felt my cheek with the back of her hand. Under any other circumstances, this would have been an occasion to fake a cough and force a thermometer into the hot berry filling of my Pop-Tart, but there was no time for fake-outs today. Summer was coming, and time was of the essence.

Dog tired, I dragged myself to school. I honestly don't know how some people get by on less than eight hours' sleep. My life requires a certain amount of energy, and that day I did not have it. To make matters worse, there's a regular freight train that crosses my route to school, and if I didn't pace my walk just right, that train would cut me off, and there would be nothing to do but sit myself on a crashed automobile in the scrap yard and count the boxcars go by. One time there were four engines and seventy-nine cars. I was a full ten minutes late to school on that day. Of course, the truth of my tardiness was uninteresting, so I dressed the story up a little for Miss Ballast's ears.

I told her that a wild-eyed hobo jumped straight off the morning freight and chased me all through the scrap yard, demanding that I give him body parts. My own, not from the wrecked cars. Eventually, I told

Schooley/McCorkle

Miss Ballast, I'd managed to get into a sideswiped International Harvester and lock the doors, while the hobo howled and beat on the truck with his fists, until blood sprayed on the windshield, hiding his hideous face from me completely. This went on a spell, but there was no denying that the folks at International Harvester make a fine product, even with the side all pushed in. That hobo was no match for American manufacturing superiority. Miss Ballast always seemed to like it when I added in something positive about America, and seeing as how I'd missed the Pledge, I figured this detail would go over especially well. I didn't think it would hurt, at any rate.

The whole class was listening by then, so I sensed that it was time to bring my tale to an end. "The hobo gave up not five minutes ago," I told everyone. "He caught up with his train, and the last thing I saw was him hanging off the caboose, waving a red finger at me and hissing, 'Next time, Sonny, your liver is mine.'"

I thought the class particularly enjoyed that last part, but Miss Ballast just squinted at me for a second, and then finally said, "We don't say 'hobo,' Peter. We say indigent, unfortunate, or homeless." I hated it when she called me by my proper name, but I guessed it wouldn't do for a professional to call me Liar.

But on the day after Justine first came to school, either the train was late or I was on time, because I crossed the tracks without any incident from fictional attackers.

I got to class just before the bell, so I didn't have time to fully recon the room for Justine's position. I imagined that this was a military operation, in honor of her daddy's occupation, with me holding a state-of-the-art electronic tracker gizmo, with a moving red dot to indicate Justine. I'd track her cool and steady, always keeping a safe two clicks behind in the brush. Whatever two clicks meant, but I'd heard it in a movie, and it seemed appropriate for this scenario I was cooking up.

But then she'd activate her superscrambler, and my tracker would turn into the world's most expensive paperweight. "The bogey is RIGHT ON TOP OF YOU!" my corporal or sergeant or whatever would scream, but by then it would be too late and Justine would get the drop on me and I'd make an idiot of myself again. Which is pretty much what happened, minus the clicks, scramblers, and such.

I'll cut right through the suspense: My fly was open. Full frontal tighty-whitey. Justine wasn't the first person to notice it, but she was surely the second, thanks to her proximity to Walter Weedbinder.

"XYZ, XYZ," Walter shrieked with his annoyingly outdoor voice, and pointed at me. I'd never had much time for Walter under any condition, but I have to say, at that moment he was just plain lucky I *wasn't* outfitted for military action. Justine looked embarrassed for me, which was preferable to her joining the pointers and laughers. Still, I knew that there was no recovering from that setback on that day, so I'd just have to regroup on the next.

Chapter FOUR

Wednesday.

Day three of Liar held hostage by hormones.

Though I had not yet reached "now or never" conditions, time was getting short. I actually fell asleep early the night before, exhaustion winning out over emotional torment. I got to school early, and I staged the scene to come. I'd have one leg propped up on my chair, and I'd lean rakishly on my elbow, chatting up some dialogue-less supporting player. Perhaps I'd have a Little Debbie Double Chocolate Swiss Cake Roll loosely gripped in my free hand, and I'd gesture with it like a lit cigar when I wanted to emphasize my point. The extra would laugh on cue, giving the arriving Justine the impression that I had just made the most funny comment ever heard at Faulkner Middle School. I even got Walter Weedbinder to play the part of the laughing boy. He had practice from the day before, and he owed me.

Sadly, this little play was woefully under-rehearsed. I hadn't counted on Justine actually getting caught by the train and coming in late. But she was new and obviously didn't know the mysterious rhythms of Kudzu like I did. That's why she needed me; she just didn't know it.

Soon enough, Walter got tired of laughing at me, which was a change of pace from the previous day. So he drifted over to the whiteboard and played with the wipe-away spray. I figured all was not lost. I could still look like an intellectual with that Little Debbie Swiss Cake in my hand.

The later Justine got to be, the more melted the swiss cake's outer chocolate shell became. Yet it was critical to my scenario that I scarcely pay attention to that jauntily held Little Debbie Double Chocolate Swiss Cake Roll. It was a prop, not a player. By the time the bell rang, whole sheets of chocolate had peeled away from the rolled cake core and fallen to the floor. Or so I thought.

What had really happened to that chocolate was that it had fallen onto Justine's chair. So the last thing she needed, being already late from the unexpected freight train, was to sit on top of a mess of melted chocolaty coating. Unfortunately, this happened on the day she'd dressed for the season in white culottes. Walter, of course, was the first to notice her brown bottom. She went red-faced, and I tried to look at her sympathetically, as if to say, "Hey, I've been there. Let's bond over our mutual hatred of Walter Weedbinder." But the effect was ruined by the fact that I was still casually dangling a now naked Little Debbie cake.

Thursday. Day four.

Thermometer in the Pop-Tart and I stayed in bed. Time was all that could heal the Little Debbie incident now.

Friday. Day five.

The day of last chances.

Schooley/McCorkle

Now that I'd had time to put the whole Little Debbie disaster in perspective, I decided this was the classic case of life dealing me some lemons, and I just needed to get squeezing. First of all, it wasn't really my fault. If there's one life skill you should have by middle school, it's to know that you always check out your chair before you sit in it. One baloney, cheese, extra mayo on my drawers in first grade was all it took to teach me.

One of the advantages of a whole day to ponder the angles was that I could see that blaming Justine was a nonstarter, given how little time I had to work with. It was then that a brilliant, crazy idea hit. I'd take the blame and I'd apologize.

It was time to make me some lemonade.

Chapter FIVE

I waited until the end of the school day. The end of the school year. The end of my life, if I couldn't get Justine to forgive and/or forget.

On one level I was lucky. With only a week in our new school, Justine hadn't really bonded with any of the toxic cliques yet. Sure there was the sense of common ground that other pretty girls shared with her. They checked her out and nodded and smiled as if to say, "You're good enough, but we can't rush this." The next year she would be welcomed fully into the hot chick superclique, and my chance of ever getting near her would be less than zero. I had backed myself into a corner. There was only one chance out, and the time had come.

Following her into the parking lot, I waited until the crowd thinned to make my move. I'd done enough public damage that week that I might have been going down in flames, but I was going to do it with dignity.

"Justine." I called her name as loud and clear as I could muster. For a moment it was an out-of-body view as I saw myself from above, looking small and scared and silly. She turned. Now I was floating above both of us. I felt like I was watching Mothra about to pound Godzilla into a power station.

Justine said, "What?"

Words had always been my friend. The right words always kept me from getting beat up or grounded. On that day, when I'd needed the right words more than life itself, words let me down. The best I could come up with was, "I'm sorry you sat on my Little Debbie."

"Whatever," Justine said back. But she said it softly and with forgiveness in her voice.

So far so good.

I noticed she was heading toward a Ford Taurus with a base parking tag and a bumper sticker that said

BE ALL YOU CAN BE on it. I intended to heed that bumper sticker's advice.

"Maybe I could show you around Kudzu some—"

Her old man in the Ford rolled down the window and shouted, "C'mon, Justy. We need to stop by the PX and pick your ma up some groceries."

She kind of shrugged at me, got in the car and drove off. Soon she would be behind the orange gate at the base, in for a summer of cheap chocolate. If indeed she could ever look at chocolate again after the Little Debbie culottes. Me, I would be paying full price at the Piggly Wiggly and dreaming of two star-crossed kids and what might have been.

It didn't work out that way.

A week later I was at our Piggly Wiggly, picking up some emergency pie supplies for Momma, on account of a paragraph in some food magazine that said she made the best sweet potato pie in the world. The avalanche of orders caught her short of taters and tins, so I had to round up what I could in town while she waited for a fresh wholesale

Schooley/McCorkle

shipment to show up in a few days. The good part of this was that Momma was so busy mashing and baking that she didn't have time to cook supper, so I got to eat restaurant food and barbecue take-out all week long. If it were not for the big old hole in my heart, the summer would have been shaping up not half-bad.

And then I saw Justine. She was there by herself too. It seemed that the base store didn't have everything. Like a certain shampoo and some types of fresh vegetables, I noticed as I studied her cart. She caught me looking, and unexpectedly she smiled.

"Hey, Liar, what are you up to?" she said. I was surprised that she had seemingly come to accept my nickname without a judgmental tone, considering her first impression. And second impression too, for that matter. Momma always said that my friendly face made people want to forgive me against their best judgment, so I guess that's what was working for me in the Piggly Wiggly.

As to Justine's question, I didn't have time to come up with anything better than the truth. "Haulin' about a ton of sweet taters for my momma," I answered, trying to at least shade the task as somewhat heroic.

Justine actually seemed interested in Momma's pie business and my family's Yankee roots. I think she liked that I had big-city blood in me.

"I lived near New York once," Justine said. She'd lived in a lot of places, I found out. We talked about what we were doing with our summers, which had been cumulatively unimpressive so far.

We hit a quiet patch. Piggly Wiggly conversations are never exactly deep and long, I figured. I ran through a million possible things to say. From her view it probably looked like I was having a stroke.

Justine touched her face and remarked, "Sure is hot out there lately." The weather! Why hadn't I thought of that? That's when she brought up my last-day-of-school offer to show her around. Now, I replayed that moment in my head a million times and was pretty sure that she must not have heard me because her Daddy was telling her to get a move on. But somehow she had heard me, and now she was standing right there in the Piggly Wiggly freezer section, smiling and saying "That would be really nice of you."

If more tender words have ever been spoken, I haven't heard them.

Chapter SIX

Now, nobody was calling what we were about to do a date, but having wasted a week beating around the bush and not getting anywhere, I was determined to make good use of time on this second chance. While I tried to fall asleep the night before I was going to see her, I invented a hundred different itineraries for my day with Justine, but every one ended with a kiss. She might be surprised by it at first, but she'd think about it for a minute and decide it was a good thing. That much could be set in ink. I knew it. I swore it. Maybe she'd even kiss me right back.

Then I woke up.

It was raining. Not a good sign. My outdoor tour

would have to be rethought. Justine's father, the army man, dropped her off at ten. He seemed nice enough, but I could tell he was looking to trip me up. I didn't tell him that I was called Liar. That was need-to-know information, and he didn't need to know it just yet. It's not like he asked if I had any aliases. I don't think he was as impressed as his girl about my folks being Yankees. Momma gave him a pie, though, so that didn't hurt any.

We went to the bowling lanes first. Our lane was warped a little from the humidity, but we weren't keeping score anyway. We laughed at each other's gutter balls. Things were feeling A-OK. It was like we could actually be friends, which was a possibility that I hadn't considered until then. I'd been too occupied planning for that kiss.

Lunch was at the Pig Stand. I had a slaw dog. She had a salad. The Pig Stand is not exactly known for their salads, but she didn't remark about it in the negative. The milk shakes were thick and cold and good. My numb lips would need time to thaw. I wanted the kiss to be one for the ages.

The sun came out. We wandered down Main, past the scrap yard, and into the woods. I told her I knew just about every kind of bird, bug, and tree in those woods, and she seemed keen to test me. I pointed out a yellow warbler in a longleaf pine. A spotted sandpiper hollered out from the thick shade of a willow oak. My daddy made it his business to know everything and try to teach it to me.

I was on such a roll that it was a shame I ran out of birds and trees I actually knew and started to make species up. She called me on the "jailbird in the Christmas tree." It was clear that things could take a turn at that point, so I knew it was time. I licked my lips. I think she noticed. But I soldiered on, feeling like she'd think that an admirable trait. I leaned close to her. She looked surprised.

What I couldn't know, since I was so fixed on the moment, was that she was looking past me at a large ball of fire in the sky, streaking toward us.

She tackled me into the wet dirt. I had a millisecond to think that I was the luckiest twelve-year-old who'd ever lived, when the ground quaked.

Not in a good way either. It was then that I lifted my head enough to push Justine's hair out of my face and see, not fifteen feet from us, a crater in the forest floor, filled with steam and smoke.

Chapter SEVEN

Under normal conditions the day would have ended awkwardly when Justine pushed me into the mud. But as the smoke cleared from the crater and we crept closer to its center, it became obvious that the day had just taken a seriously peculiar turn.

Around the edges of the crater were bits of wire and electronic-looking stuff; in the center was the thing from which they'd broken off. It was about the size of a VW Beetle, or maybe a Mini Cooper. Not that there were any Mini Coopers in Kudzu, but I'd seen them in commercials. The craft was burnt and banged up from its atmospheric fall, but it still had enough size to it that I was pretty sure somebody could still be alive inside. Or some*thing*.

Now, I am blessed with uncommon imagination. This is pretty handy in a little town where nothing much ever happens. But the spectacle before me was real, and my imagination froze solid. Justine and me were suddenly in a science fiction movie. I tried to sneeze, hoping that the spray of germs would kill the aliens in that ship before they could come out, lasers blazing. I wondered if there were ships plopping down all over Earth, ruining other guys' first kisses.

Justine got even closer to the thing. Blue hot metal edges were starting to cool to black. She picked up a branch and swiped at the powdery char on the surface. I tried to be supportive and protect things from the outer edge of the crater. She called me closer. I kept sneezing, and she didn't see that I was trying to save her life. In fact, she said "Knock it off" and pointed to the area she'd cleaned off. It was a metal plate, engraved with a bunch of circles to indicate a solar system much like our own. She brushed some more, and two figures emerged; it looked like a man and a woman. Embarrassing, because they were both buck naked and all that implies. I tried to ignore the nudity in favor of more general conclusions.

"These aliens look almost human!" I said.

Justine pointed to an American flag etched on the side. "And patriotic, too," she cracked.

"More like diabolically clever," I said. I knew that TV signals bounced around in space forever, so I was sure aliens were quite familiar with Old Glory if they'd ever caught Fox News.

She shook her head. She wasn't ready to accept that it was an alien spaceship. I, on the other hand, believed. This was a big event, and we owned it. I thought about who I should give my first, exclusive interview to. The problem with real news shows is they would just come here and film me. If I went on *Oprah*, I'd have to go to her. They'd probably put us up in a fancy hotel. I remembered that she came from Chicago. I had been there when I was little and had gone to the aquarium and to the museum that has a gigantic heart you can walk right though, pretending you're a blood cell. I must have been only five, but that big heart left an impression.

Justine would go to Chicago too, of course. We were in this together. Maybe she'd be in the room next to ours in the fancy, Oprah-approved hotel. I could picture the whole thing. We'd be the toasts of the town. I'd take her to the heart. Maybe I'd finally kiss her there. I couldn't think of anything more romantic than having your first kiss in a heart the size of a house, with the sound of fake blood thumping all around you.

Justine lacked my powers of prophecy, for while I was planning our whole Windy City adventure, she realized that her father was coming for her in ten minutes. Apparently, Army Dad didn't take kindly to tardiness. I needed time to think anyway. Justine helped me cover the crash with branches and leaves until it looked like a crazy beaver had built his dam away from anything actually worth a dam. We swore each other to secrecy and said we'd meet up again in the morning. This was working out. Maybe the aliens had interrupted my big move, but they had hooked me up for a second date without even having to ask.

I was dying to tell someone else about the event,

but I doubted even friends or family would buy it, coming from me. Maybe if I hadn't put the town on alert for an alien invasion the previous summer, I could have actually told them about the crash. How was I to know that my best lie would come true, even if it was a year later? When I'd first started telling stories, everyone and their sister told me the one about the boy who cried wolf. I hated that story. After all, it was pretty stupid and unbelievable. I mean, what were the chances of a real wolf coming in there on that boy?

My current situation would seem to indicate the chances were better than I had previously thought.

It was still light out when Daddy and I went out for fried pickles and pulled pork sandwiches. Momma was continuing her sweet-potato-pie marathon. All through the meal I thought about telling Daddy that we are not alone. But I knew it would just send Momma into the psychology books, and she had too many sweet potatoes to mash to be worrying about my mental state.

There was no good TV that night. And besides, no

Schooley/McCorkle

summer reruns could compete with the real thing waiting for me in the woods. I started to think ahead to the next day and what Justine and me would do once we uncovered it. It was then that I realized I didn't have a clue. What we needed was an expert. A scientific genius.

Chapter EIGHT

Bobby Ray Dobbs's house was in a development called Shady Brook. I'm not sure why it was called that, because all the trees in there were puny as could be, and there was no brook, either. Even though it was only about twenty-five houses big, Shady Brook was a prestigious part of town because all of the houses were new, with three-car garages and central air-conditioning.

Mrs. Dobbs seemed confused when she answered the door. I doubted Bobby Ray got visitors very often, maybe ever. The house was as cool as a crypt inside. No wonder Bobby Ray didn't go outside much. I wouldn't either if my room was refrigerated. Even with the supercooled air the inside of the Dobbses' house smelled kind of funny, like the hermetic seal had kept in some cooking smells that should have been let out days before. Everything was neat and new, but the smell kept things from being too perfect.

If his momma was confused by my unannounced evening appearance, Bobby Ray was positively suspicious. I found him on his computer, typing furiously. He was in some sort of scientific chat room, and he was holding his own in a discussion about quarks or something. It was a safe bet that the others involved had no idea that BobDobbs42 was twelve years old and kept a bottle of disinfectant next to his machine so he could spray down his keyboard every fifteen minutes or so.

Mrs. Dobbs dropped me off at Bobby Ray's room by announcing, "A friend has come for a visit." He and I both knew that this wasn't true, but we let her believe it for our own individual reasons. Him because he was curious about what would bring the kid who'd once claimed to be Finnish royalty to his room on a Tuesday night. Me because I needed to tell someone who would want to believe me.

One look around Bobby Ray's room and I knew I had come to the right place. First of all, there was the computer. It wasn't like people in Kudzu didn't have computers, but most houses had one that everyone had to share. Nobody I knew had one right by his bed with broadband Internet and everything. Bobby Ray's walls were covered with posters of the kind you'd usually only see in science class. There was a history of the space program, from the monkey-nauts to today. There was a colorful depiction of the big bang and one with the solar system in 3-D. There was a bookcase filled with *Star Wars* junk that he obviously hadn't even played with, because every-thing was still in its plastic package. Maybe he feared germs from the Chinese toy factories. He even had painted glow-in-the-dark stars on his ceiling, accurately depicting the constellations visible in the Kudzu summer sky. And for the cherry on it all, on top of his computer there was an action figure, if you could call a hunched-over little guy in a wheel-chair an action figure.

No doubt about it, Bobby Ray was one freaky kid.

After his momma left us, Bobby Ray pumped some Purell onto his palm and rubbed it in for a good long time. He had a Sam's Club–size bottle of the stuff on his nightstand. I tried to make small talk and asked him about that wheelchair guy action figure.

"So does that chair transform into a robot or something cool?" I asked.

He looked at me like I was dumb as dirt. "That's Stephen W. Hawking," he said, in a humoring-the-dodo way.

The name rang a bell, sort of. "What's his powers again?" I said like I knew full well but just happened to forget.

"Only the greatest theoretical physicist since Einstein."

I didn't feel so bad for not knowing him then. "Oh, yeah. That guy," I lied. Still, supergenius or no, it didn't seem like grounds for making an action figure. Then again, my mind hadn't been so much on toys of late.

"Whatcha doin' here, Liar?" Bobby Ray finally had to know.

So I told him. I was a little shocked that he seemed to believe every word. No one else would have, but he actually had a few books on the subject of UFO's. We paged through them, looking at blurry pictures of lights in the sky, like I was trying to finger some creep in a mug book. Nothing exactly matched.

The mystery only deepened, and Bobby Ray was hooked. He agreed to meet up with Justine and me in the morning to try and figure out what was what in the woods.

Chapter NINE

The next morning Justine got dropped off again at ten o'clock straight up. It was clear that her daddy was new to town, because nobody in Kudzu is on time two days in a row. Bobby Ray sure wasn't. I guess it was a big step for him, going outside, with people. But he was as curious as I was, so whatever he had to do to talk himself into coming out might have taken some time, but he found the strength. I pitied and admired him. His lateness was a chance for me to prepare Justine about what to expect. There were the wet-naps, of course. But even after only one week in school, she knew about those.

There were other, less obvious, Bobby Ray quirks. He would always touch a doorknob three times before he could open it. He'd touch his nose, then his ear, then his nose again, over and over for no good reason. Even in the heat of the day, he'd wear only long sleeves and his shirt buttoned up to his Adam's apple. No wonder he barely left his room in the summer. He was already overheated when he got to my house at ten thirty. When I heard the front doorknob rattle three times, I didn't need to check to see who was there.

We met him on the porch. Bobby Ray came equipped with a camera and a thermometer. It was a digital thermometer that you'd use on the grill to see if your chicken was cooked enough to not kill you. But it looked pretty scientific in this context. With barely a word spoken the three of us headed into the woods.

Bobby Ray was out of breath and freaking out about spiders that he didn't see but just knew were touching him, when we got back to the scene of the alien invasion. When he had finally stopped hyperventilating, I had bad news.

The spacecraft was gone. Not just gone, but it was like it had never been there. Our bogus beaver dam was gone too, along with the crater. The ground was smoothed over in such a way that you would never have known there'd been an invasion if you hadn't almost been flattened by it.

"Ha, ha, ho, very funny," Bobby Ray whined in a way that suggested maybe people had done something like this to him on a previous occasion.

Justine ignored him and got a worried look. "This is a cover-up. And we're the only ones who know about it." She sat on a rock and spoke in a serious tone. Her father had once been stationed at Area 51, Justine said. And even though he hadn't had clearance to see the really top secret alien technologies and biological samples, what he *had* seen was plenty bizarre.

Bobby Ray's left eye twitched, which I think meant that he was interested. You could never really tell with Bobby Ray, since everything looked like a nervous breakdown from the spectator's position.

"You know how they said it was just a big old weather balloon that crashed in Roswell, New Mexico?" Justine continued.

"What—*gulp*—was it?" Bobby Ray had to know. His eye was fluttering like a moth.

Justine paused for dramatic effect. I was liking her more and more. She could really put over a story. Just as she was about to spill the secret of Roswell, a branch cracked right behind Bobby Ray, and he nearly had a heart attack right there. He spun around, and there was a big man in a black Windbreaker, sporting an extremely unpleasant expression.

"What brings you kids out here?" the scary man asked, with a smile that somehow made him look meaner.

"We're Boy Scouts," I lied. Playing off Justine's dumbfounded expression, I added, "Except her; she's a girl."

Looking back, I realize it wasn't one of my better fabrications, but the guy looked like he meant business. I had a feeling if he knew Justine and me were witnesses to the invasion, we'd end up in some windowless room, hooked up to state-of-the-art lie detector machines. In other words, my worst nightmare.

He asked us more questions, and my lies got more convincing as I relaxed and got back into my zone. I knew one thing: I couldn't let Bobby Ray get a word in, or we were all goners. It was going pretty well too, but I got distracted. I watched an old blackbird pick at the mud where the crater had been. At first it looked like she was pulling out a worm, but as she flew off, I could see that it was a scrap of wire. Her nest was high in the branches of a swamp gum tree. As the man grilled me, I couldn't stop staring at that nest. In it, glinting in the sun, was a gold compact disc. I had a hunch where that old bird had found it.

Lucky for us, while I was bird-watching, Justine picked up the slack with our interrogator. She actually started to question *him*. I focused back on her just in time to appreciate what an awesome member of the female species Justine was.

Justine's reverse play actually seemed to work. The man gave us each a business card. Ed Hemet, NSA. He was all the way from Virginia.

Bobby Ray finally spoke. "You misspelled NASA."

Ed Hemet ignored him and said, "Give me a call if

you find anything unusual." I had to pry my eyes from that gold CD because I knew that it would surely fit Ed Hemet's definition.

A black SUV crept in behind Ed, and the driver looked like he could be Ed's brother. Our interrogator shot us a gut-check stare, and the two drove off toward the main road.

Justine turned to Bobby Ray to explain, "NSA, National Security Agency. This is big."

Bobby Ray truly didn't understand what was going on, and neither did I really, but I thought I knew more than he did. For reasons I can't explain, I was sure that the gold CD would crack everything wide open.

I had Bobby Ray give me a boost into that swamp gum tree. Every second that my muddy foot was cupped in his hands was like decades to the poor guy. As soon as I lifted myself up into the branches, he had his wetnap out. Of course, no sooner had he scrubbed up than I had the CD and needed help down.

The CD didn't have a label as such, but it did have

some stuff etched into it. There was some kind of diagram that Bobby Ray studied, and he said it looked like it was showing someone how to build a CD player. Why would anyone have to build a CD player?

Justine had a portable one in her backpack. Bobby Ray said that if this were an alien CD, the chances of it working on a player from Wal-Mart were pretty slim. I popped it in anyway. I figured, what's the worst that could happen?

Then I instantly thought of a worst thing. Some sort of alien mind-control signal, maybe.

I figured I'd let Bobby Ray listen first, just in case.

"Here you go, Bobby Ray," I said. "You stand a better chance of deciphering alien than Justine or me."

Bobby Ray looked doubtful, but the nerd centers in his brain must have blocked out his usual fear response. He took the headphones from me and held them a germ-safe distance from his ears. Even from where I was sitting I could tell that it was not an alien broadcast. It was music Daddy listened to, the Beatles. We skipped through the tracks. There was some classical stuff. Some old blues lady. An Elvis tune. Even "Lose Yourself" from Eminem, the clean version. I figured we'd found somebody's iTunes mix, but Bobby Ray wasn't so sure. He wanted to take the disc home and play it in his computer. It was the etching on it that got to him. It didn't look like a homemade rip job. That was fine with me. I had plans with Justine to consider, and the sooner we got out of the intrigue mode, the better all around.

Chapter TEN

As we walked back to Bobby Ray's house, a storm blew up out of nowhere. It wasn't raining too bad, but the thunder was something awful. I thought Bobby Ray would jump out of his skin with every crack. A few summers back a freshman at the college had gotten hit by lightning and almost died. For a month after, we all talked about whether he'd had it coming. I came down on the side of yes, on account that he'd been a fool to climb up the old water tower during the worst of it. His action confirmed my suspicions about the caliber of student enrolled in Daddy's college.

The sky opened up good just as we got to Shady Brook. There were no trees of a height to draw in the lightning, but we ran for the house anyway. The cold of the air-conditioning felt arctic when we ran inside in our wet clothes. My teeth chattered like a windup toy.

Mrs. Dobbs seemed giddy that Bobby Ray had brought home not just me but a fine-looking, if soaked, girl. This was obviously an event that lacked precedent. Mrs. Dobbs grabbed us some towels, and we got as dry as we could. She offered to throw our clothes in the dryer and lend us a couple of her bathrobes to warm up in. Both Justine and I decided that we'd rather be freezing than play out that scenario. Even though we were dying to get into Bobby Ray's room and pop that CD into his computer, Mrs. Dobbs insisted on fixing up a mess of lunch. We sat at the kitchen table while she set out egg salad sandwiches and sweet tea.

I was about to grab a sandwich, when Mrs. Dobbs ordered us to the sink to wash our hands. Of course, Bobby Ray had already taken care of that as soon as he'd gotten back into the house, but Justine and I scrubbed up. I think I could have handled it myself, but Bobby Ray's mom insisted on squeezing a giant gob of Dawn antibacterial soap onto my hands, as though she had a personal grudge against germs. It was unsettling. Lightning flashed through her kitchen curtains and Mrs. Dobbs jumped to the spigot to kill the water. She said that lightning could travel right through the pipe and strike us down there in her kitchen. I started to see where Bobby Ray's problems took root.

The lunch was all right on the better-than-tofu scale, but watching Bobby Ray and his mother flinch with every thunder boom got old quick. Plus, the pressure to eat everything she laid out was too much. She'd cut up a watermelon and opened a bag of chips, too. It was like she was determined to make up for all the years that Bobby Ray hadn't had any friends over. Maybe she thought we would spread the word, and other kids from school would start coming over for the buffet. I got the feeling she worried about Bobby Ray a little too much for her or his own good.

As we ate our egg salad, Mrs. Dobbs leaned against the stove and tried to make small talk. I was getting the feeling that Bobby Ray wasn't the only person who didn't get out of the house much. It seemed that Mr. Dobbs traveled a lot, and Mrs. Dobbs found that taking care of the house and Bobby Ray as "practically a single mother" took everything she had to give. Why she was telling her life story to two kids she'd just met, I had no idea. And I'd thought my momma was high-strung.

Finally Mrs. Dobbs disappeared for a minute, and we thought that lunch was over. But just as we were folding our paper plates into the trash, she came in from the garage with a mile-high red velvet cake. Why she just happened to have this cake was a mystery. You wouldn't exactly call the woman petite, though, so she may have baked it for personal use. I've never been a huge fan of red velvet cake because I've never been able to figure out what I'm supposed to taste. I get vanilla cake, chocolate cake, and lemon cake. But what flavor is red velvet? I hated it when I couldn't figure out things like that.

I was stuck eating it anyway, and so was Justine. I don't think she had ever even had red velvet cake before, so she was even more in the dark than I was.

I told her it was made with red velvet ants when she'd put the first forkful into her mouth. She almost choked on her cake. An unintended consequence of my highly developed lying skills is that sometimes even my jokes sound like I'm serious.

By the time we got to Bobby Ray's room, we were so stuffed that we practically forgot about why we were there. At least we were half-dry by then, even if the rain was coming down in buckets outside.

"I'm going to put the CD in the computer drive now." Bobby Ray narrated himself as though the event were being recorded for future generations. But just as he touched the button, thunder shook the house, and he fell back like he'd been struck by a gigavolt. For a pretty new, pretty fancy house the walls *did* seem awfully thin on the big booms. But of all of us, you'd think that the boy who lived in the room would be the most used to it.

Bobby Ray clutched his heart and looked at us to see if we were in sympathetic hysterics. Disappointed that we were calm, he got back to work and put the CD in the computer drawer. With dramatic flourish he started clicking things with his mouse until the drawer automatically shut. If it had been me, I would have just whacked the sucker closed with my knee, but to each his own, I guess.

First an antivirus warning came up on the screen, saying that the new disc was being scanned. I thought that this was good, just in case the whole CD thing was an alien plot to hack into the Internet. I was relieved to see the scan give the all clear. Next, a box came up on the screen and a program-loading bar started to move across. Apparently even aliens used Microsoft.

When a picture finally showed up, it was of something called the Vespucci probe. The name rang no bells for me, but Bobby Ray pointed to one of the space posters on his wall. It showed a bunch of small satellite-looking things labeled DEEP SPACE PROBES. Sure enough, one of them was labeled VESPUCCI. But I figured that it must be a different Vespucci, because the little box below the one on the poster said it wouldn't even be launched for another year. Something, besides Bobby Ray, wasn't quite right here.

Schooley/McCorkle

"Maybe it was some kind of a test launch," Justine guessed.

"Then I'm guessing it flunked the test," I said.

"Are you sure this is what the crashed craft looked like?" Bobby Ray asked, tapping on the screen with his knuckle for emphasis.

We stared at the probe on the screen and the one on the poster for a minute. Justine and I both agreed that the crashed thing in the woods could have looked a lot like this Vespucci probe before its distressing journey. Then, to cinch it, the words "Property of the United States of America" came up on Bobby Ray's computer. This was a disappointing development. Finding a message from aliens was a big deal. Finding a message from the United States government would more than likely just get us into trouble. I thought it was probably sending an instant message to Ed Hemet right then, and we'd be surrounded by Feds in five minutes.

I guess I shouldn't have said the part about the Feds out loud. Bobby Ray got all shook up and scurried to yank the plug on his cable modem. Just as he grabbed the wire, the brightest, loudest, most awesome lightning strike hit "one Mississippi" close. A spark flew from the modem. Bobby Ray screamed. The electricity to the whole neighborhood went dead. Mrs. Dobbs came up the stairs like a runaway train, building up speed without a proper distance to brake. She fell into the room and tripped over Bobby Ray on the floor. They both let out animal sounds. It was a real human comedy.

All I could think about was that I wasn't going to be on *Oprah* and I wasn't going to kiss Justine inside the giant heart. At the rate things were going, I wondered if we'd ever be more than friends, period.

We all sat around in Bobby Ray's room for a while. It wasn't like it was pitch black or anything, but the room only had one window and the sky outside was muddied by clouds. The effect was gloomy. We couldn't talk freely because Mrs. Dobbs was sticking around for no obvious reason. The storm, the blackout, the visitors; it was too much for the woman.

I'd just gotten dried out and used to the freezing air-conditioning, and now here it was off and the house was getting hotter and stuffier by the minute. The Vespucci mystery would have to wait because I needed to get out of there. I think Justine felt the same way, because she pretty much leapt at my lead when I made up a story about getting home to help my daddy change the oil in his car. If Mrs. Dobbs had known my daddy, she'd have seen right through the excuse. Unlike most of the men in Kudzu, Daddy believes in paying a specialist to do anything more complicated than changing a lightbulb. And half the time Momma does that chore. It's not that Daddy's lazy, just aware of his limitations.

We left Bobby Ray in his warm dark house. I sure hoped his momma wouldn't explode from all the commotion, because I would have felt partially responsible. The rain was letting up, and it felt good at that point, anyway. Walking out of the neighborhood, Justine spotted the source of the troubles: a giant maple split in two by lightning. A branch had knocked down the main power line into Shady Brook. It was probably the only tree that they'd left standing when they'd bulldozed in to build those houses. The severed power line sparked and hissed on the wet grass. I wondered how long before the county power company would get out there to fix it up. How long would Bobby Ray and his nervous mother have to sit in the dark? Would she ever open her windows?

"It's funny how life goes" is all I could think to say on the subject to Justine. I don't think she even knew what I was referring to. I thought about kissing her there in the warm rain, but after the giant-heart kiss plan, everything else just seemed too humdrum. It was times like that when I felt the town of Kudzu was just too small for me.

Chapter **ELEVEN**

The next morning, Bobby Ray called and woke me up school-day early. I asked if he had ever popped open his window and aired out that room, but he talked over me. He said they'd finally fixed his power in the middle of the night. He was sleeping when the lights came back on in his room and snapped him out of a dream. I asked him if it was a good dream or a bad one, but he wasn't calling for conversation; he had a story to tell. It struck me that he didn't have any real friends to call, so he woke me up instead. I couldn't help but feel sorry for him. As much as I wanted to go back to sleep, I listened out of common courtesy.

Bobby Ray went on to say that his computer booted back up when the power did. A voice came out saying

"Greetings from Earth." The first time was in English, then the CD kept saying it in just about every language you could think of. So Bobby Ray started to play with his computer, right then and there in the middle of the night. There were pictures of a bunch of inconsequential stuff. The ocean. A baby. The Grand Canyon. A car. Interesting if you're E.T., maybe, but not particularly so if you were born and raised on the planet.

But just when Bobby Ray was getting sleepy, he noticed that the CD had a whole section with front pages from the *New York Times*. Thousands of them.

Every once in a while Daddy would bring the *New York Times* home from the college and sit on the porch and read every word of it. I looked one over once, but I didn't see the attraction. Stinking Yankee boosters didn't even print the scores of the Dixon County Catfish. Sure they were only minor league, but if the paper had space for stories about beach parties on Long Island, you'd think they could squeeze in a line or two to cover the Catfish. Maybe a human interest story about the guy who shoots T-shirts out of a cannon while wearing a big foam catfish costume. I had started a rumor at school that the guy had to wear the costume as a condition of parole. It might have been true, for all I know. The man in the catfish suit guarded his privacy. Maybe that's why the *New York Times* never saw fit to feature him.

I hadn't had breakfast yet, so I was a little slow when Bobby Ray said the next thing.

"The dates on the papers . . ." He lowered his voice, trying to sound ominous but not really transcending nasal. "They start in 1900 and go until September."

"Of what year?" I said, thinking more about hotcakes and berry syrup than what he was saying.

"*This* year, Liar."

"You mean last year, right?" I corrected the genius. "It's not even June. We got the whole summer ahead of us." I would have said that even if it were late July. It was my habit to insist the whole summer was still ahead, even if the dark specter of the Wal-Mart back-to-school ads had signaled otherwise. I may be mostly a liar, but I'm an optimist, too.

"September of this year, Liar." He spoke slowly for my benefit, "As . . . in . . . the . . . *future*." Bobby Ray seemed determined to prove that he had popped his cork completely. Just goes to show you how nothing but straight As can eat at a man's soul eventually.

"How could they have future newspapers on that CD, Bobby Ray?" I regretted ever extending the hand of friendship to this sad boy.

"Come over. See it with your own eyes," he said, then he hung up.

It wasn't like I had big plans for the day, but the last thing I wanted was to have to choke down egg salad and red velvet cake again. It occurred to me that Bobby Ray's story was so crazy that I'd better tell Justine to meet me there, so she could give a second opinion.

When I called Justine, I just said, "Bobby Ray's lost his mind. Meet me there."

She had questions, but I thought if I repeated too much, she'd start to ponder about my sanity. The complication was that her daddy was actually being all he could be that day, and that didn't include driving Justine over. Luckily, Momma had shipped the last of her big pie rush and was willing to drive me to the base to pick up Justine. She said she felt like she was running a taxi service sometimes. Maybe so, but a genuine taxi driver wouldn't have asked so dang many questions about this "girl you're suddenly so interested in." And he wouldn't have acted like he was getting all emotional about his "baby sprouting into a man." I told Momma that I was just trying to be neighborly since Justine was new at school. Momma flashed me a weird smile and said, "Uh-huh." I sunk down in my seat. A perfectly good lie didn't take. I felt like I was losing my touch.

We got to the gate, and I thought the guard might be the same one I'd tried to talk my way past on last summer's chocolate mission, but I couldn't be sure, because they all looked the same. We couldn't just wander around the base, but we were allowed into the part where people lived, not the part where they blow stuff up. There were dozens of long yellow buildings that all looked the same. Yellow seemed like an odd paint choice for the army, image-wise. Maybe they got a good deal.

Justine came running out, and I couldn't tell from where exactly. Not that I could imagine ever slipping past the guards and the razor wire to pay an unannounced visit, but I was curious to see where she lived. She was going to get in the backseat of the car, but I thought fast and pushed over so she'd sit up front with me and Momma. We were kind of squeezed tight, but I wasn't complaining.

By the time we got over to Bobby Ray's house, it was eleven fifteen. Not really lunchtime, but anything is possible from a woman who keeps an entire red velvet cake on standby. To our great relief, though, Bobby Ray was home alone. His mother was at the beauty parlor, and he said that was usually an all-day event. I had no reason to doubt him.

Bobby Ray got Justine up to date on his crackpot discovery. Even though he clicked to tomorrow's *New York Times* front page, I still thought he was pulling off the greatest lie in history. I'd told some whoppers, but never with visual aids.

Exasperated with my skeptical questions, Bobby Ray pulled a book off his shelf. He didn't have as many books as Momma and Daddy, but he had a lot more than me. Or any other normal kid, for that matter. The book was by the same guy as the wheelchair action figure, Stephen Hawking. Bobby Ray looked at the index, and went to a particular page. I never use a book's index; I just lick and flip until I find what I'm looking for. Bobby Ray and me had pretty different approaches to many things, I figured.

He showed me a drawing of a tube in space. It was called a wormhole, which sounded made-up to me, but Bobby Ray said that he believed they were real and that the Vespucci probe had actually flown through one. Unlike the genius, I had barely passed basic science, and I was lost already.

Justine kept staring at Bobby Ray's space geek poster that showed the Vespucci. "It's not even supposed to take off until next year."

"Precisely." Bobby Ray slammed his book shut.

"Precisely, what?" I asked.

"The probe will be launched next spring," he said.

"Well, they're going to have to bang out some dents, then," I said, imagining Ed Hemet doing just that.

"No." Bobby Ray explained as best he could, "The Vespucci crashed after the launch. Way after."

Both Justine and I were no closer to having a clue to what he was saying.

"The Vespucci probe will be launched next April. It will travel for maybe twenty or thirty years, leaving the Milky Way itself. It is at that point, according to my hypothesis, that the probe will be pulled into a wormhole, and when it passes through, time itself will be warped."

It was maybe the stupidest thing I'd ever heard. But I just made a neutral face, like I was letting it all sink in.

"Along the way the probe's programmed navigation gets mixed up and sends it back to the planet it came from. *Bam!* It crashes in our woods." He paused for maximum drama, then added the punch line in a half whisper that he saved for only his dweebiest pronouncements, "Before it was even launched."

Bobby Ray folded his arms smugly, like he'd just become the new all-time *Jeopardy* champ.

Justine looked at me and said, "I think Bobby Ray might be right."

I couldn't believe it. It didn't even take one to know one here; anyone could have seen that Bobby Ray was telling stories. How could Justine be buying it?

Then again, I didn't want to be odd man out and push Justine away from me and toward Bobby Ray. That would be seriously sick and wrong. I played along.

"Really," I asked with faked sincerity. "You think?"

Justine clicked the mouse, looking through the future headlines, and she said that there was no way Bobby Ray could have made all this stuff up overnight. She went back and looked at the paper for that day. There was a story about a government study on the hidden dangers of certain kinds of soap. I had heard the story earlier that morning while I was getting dressed, and, of course, it had made me think of Bobby Ray. Not that I hadn't already been pondering his sanity since he'd woken me up, but the toxic soap story had added a new dimension of irony. If he wanted to pull the scam of the century, I just couldn't picture him writing an exposé against antibacterial soap.

Still, I couldn't quite wrap my head around this wormhole business, so just to satisfy my natural suspicions I suggested that we go over to the college and compare their paper to the one on his computer. I just wanted to double check that Bobby Ray wasn't the new liar king of Kudzu.

Chapter TWELVE

I was going to call Momma's Taxi service, but Justine said that the base runs a shuttle that stops downtown and goes over to the college. Officially it's so the soldiers' families can go to the library or take a pottery class, but in reality it's more often used by the young recruits themselves to go play pool in the student center and flirt with girls that aren't in uniform.

In the summer there aren't really great prospects in that department, so when we met the van outside of the Piggly Wiggly, we had it almost to ourselves. The only other passenger was a young-looking lady who seemed like she was just riding along to get out of her yellow house for a while. Justine knew her. She whispered to me that this woman had just gotten married, and her husband had been deployed overseas the week after the wedding. I'd seen soldiers come and go from the base my whole life, but this was an angle on it that I'd never even considered. Bobby Ray was looking out the window and thinking about Lord knows what, but I just kept sneaking looks at that army bride. She was so quiet and still, it was like she didn't even notice us on the van.

I could tell we were getting close to the college, because there was a gourmet coffeehouse right outside the gates. It's the only example of its kind in Dixon County, and when they built it, a lot of people said that nobody in their right mind would pay three dollars for a cup of coffee when you could get a strong hot mug downtown at the Mason Jar Café for fifty cents. But for Momma it was like an old friend had come by for a visit. And from her mail-order pie experience, she knew all about premium pricing. She found an excuse to stop by there nearly every day the autumn it opened.

The college was in sleepy summer mode. There were a few summer classes and what they called

Schooley/McCorkle

"camps," which in my opinion were exactly the same as the classes. Daddy taught at a "writers' camp," but there was a whole lot more talking than camping. Still, it was his favorite time of year because the folks who came down for it were usually from New York or Boston, and he didn't have to grade anything.

The van dropped us off in front of the student activities center, but there wasn't much activity, or students, for that matter. The library was up on a little hill. It looked kind of like an ancient Greek temple up there, and even though I wasn't the best reader, I always liked going up the big steps and inside the huge main reading room. Kudzu's churches are mostly small, neat, and functional. They do the job without a lot of fuss, but when you went into that library, you felt like you were in a genuine sacred place. At least I did.

My appreciation for the architecture did not extend to actually knowing where to find the *New York Times* in there. I acted like I did anyway, and led Justine and Bobby Ray in a circuitous route through the stacks. It was in our wandering that we turned a corner and came across Daddy surrounded by a small circle of bald men, and women with long wild gray-streaked hair. It looked like a meeting of dentists and witches. They were in the middle of a highfalutin poetry talk. I actually listened for a second, thinking I might pick up a useful line to apply, should I ever get Justine into the giant heart in Chicago. No such luck. In the middle of windy talk about something called the poet's paradox, Daddy looked up, saw me, then went right back to his teaching as though I were invisible. I was frankly impressed by his game face. But he stopped a second later and got up and excused himself from the dentists and witches. I guess it had just taken a second for the sight of me to sink in.

"What brings you here, son?" he said, not upset, just curiously wanting the information. This put me in a paradoxical situation myself. If I told him about why we were really there, he'd for sure think it was a lie. I know I would have. So I really had no choice but to make up a lie that sounded more likely than the actual truth. It kind of took the pleasure out of lying, but I found a way to make it fun.

"My friend Bobby Ray over there is a little slow," I said.

"How so?" Daddy asked. He was a man who sweated the details. Luckily, I was good at making up details.

"Well, among other things, he has that problem where he mixes up letters and stuff," I improvised. "So I'm going to tutor him in the basics, do what I can do for the poor kid."

"I'm glad to see you putting your creative language skills to good use," Daddy said as he looked over at Bobby Ray, who was at that instant unknowingly helping me out by struggling to open a wetnap package with his teeth. When he tore off a corner, he pulled away the empty foil, leaving the white nap dangling from his mouth. I couldn't have come up with a better illustration for my story if I'd drawn it myself.

"I've got a lot of work to do," I added gravely.

Daddy looked at me like I was Mother Teresa come back. I actually felt a little good about myself and the serendipity of how my lie related to Bobby Ray's quirk. Turned out that the library really did bring out the best in me.

Daddy went back to his dental coven. Two seconds after he turned away from me, Justine grabbed my arm and shook the *New York Times* she'd found. She seemed a little superior about it, but I let it pass. It's what a boyfriend would do, I figured, and I was determined to start thinking in those terms. Anyway, I was relieved that she'd just missed Daddy, so I didn't have to add an extra character into my Bobby Ray lie.

Bobby Ray caught up a minute later. He was a little confused by an encounter he'd just had. Seemed my daddy had put a hand on his shoulder and told him, "Stay on the path, my friend. Leonardo da Vinci, Albert Einstein, and Tom Cruise all conquered dyslexia." I told him Daddy was always saying things like that out of the blue. I'm not sure Bobby Ray believed me.

"Tom Cruise is dyslexic?" Justine repeated, like it was a big news flash. I hadn't thought she was like other girls, but I guess Tom Cruise is a common female fixation denominator.

"Nobody's perfect," I said. It was beside the point to me by then anyway, because I had grabbed Bobby

Ray's printout from him and was holding it up next to the real *New York Times*.

It was a dead perfect match. The upshot of this seemed a lot bigger than a movie actor's reading problem.

It was against everything I stood for, but I was becoming a believer. Who would have thought that three kids in Kudzu would be able to read the future? The only question now was how fast we could get back to Bobby Ray's house and get started.

We raced back out to the shuttle drop-off, only to see the stupid bus pulling away. Justine and me probably could have caught it, but Bobby Ray wasn't likely to medal in the hundred-yard dash. Hitching a ride with my daddy would have taken even longer than waiting for the shuttle to loop back, so we were stuck. Sitting and waiting on the curb gave us time to ponder our discovery. I didn't say it out loud, but suddenly the *Oprah* trip seemed back on the front burner. What I did say was, "This is going to change our lives." I don't think Bobby Ray even heard me. He was in his own head, probably trying to figure out how he could call Stephen Hawking and spill his guts.

Justine looked thoughtful. She brushed her bangs back and said, "I think we have to keep this secret." Ed Hemet from the government is what worried her. "His people made the crashed probe disappear. Maybe they'd do the same thing to us."

Bobby Ray looked like he wanted to throw up or pee himself. Probably would have too, if not for the mess it would have made.

It struck me that Justine might be more than a little paranoid, but then she *was* savvy in the ways of the world. Thanks to her daddy's job, she had lived everywhere from San Diego, California, to Seoul, Korea; I figured she knew the score better than I did.

With hopeful visions of *Oprah* fading, I asked Justine why she thought Ed Hemet would care if we told anybody. Bobby Ray spoke up. He said that if we told people things that were going to happen, that could change what people would do, and that could upset the course of history itself.

"But we could be on *Oprah*," I blurted out. They

both stared at me, and I felt like a big zit. Obviously Justine couldn't have known that I was willing to risk unraveling the fabric of time in order to get an opportunity to kiss her inside a giant replica of a heart. And I'd said enough already.

Justine said, "We *could* stop something bad from happening. Warn people about a tornado or a hurricane." Justine didn't say it, but I think the *Oprah* talk was working on her.

Then Bobby Ray started talking about *Star Trek*, and I had a sinking feeling. Something about how we could violate the "prime directive" if we weren't careful. He even said we should destroy the CD and forget we'd ever found it. I was used to some level of crazy talk constantly spewing from Bobby Ray's yap, but this took the red velvet cake.

The problem was that the disc was in Bobby Ray's house, and I knew enough about the law to know possession is nine tenths of it. I would have had to either convince him or overpower him with superior force. The problem there was that I wasn't actually sure I *had* superior force. Bobby Ray may have been a brain, but he was brawny, too. Not that he was ripped or anything, but he was a few weight classes over me, so I wasn't looking to take chances that he'd Hulk out on me if I got him mad.

The situation would require finesse. I said that destroying the CD would be like Newton forgetting he'd ever gotten beaned by that famous apple. Daddy had taught me about analogies when I was seven years old, but this was the first occasion I'd ever had to use that lesson. It gave me hope that some of Daddy's other attempts at making me smart might pay off someday too.

While I was pondering this, the van pulled up. As we boarded, Bobby Ray was still trying to explain *Star Trek* science. Justine and me stopped listening when we saw that army bride, still sitting in the same seat. She didn't look at us, but I couldn't help looking at her. I thought her eyes looked kind of puffed up. Maybe she had allergies. Maybe she was thinking about things she'd have been best not to. I thought about the power to see the future. Would she want to know her future? I guessed that would depend on which way it was going to turn. I was suddenly not sure that Bobby Ray was entirely wrong.

When we got back to Bobby Ray's house, we were stopped cold by the sight of a new black SUV with a government license plate in his driveway. We went around back and peeked in the kitchen window. Ed Hemet was sitting at the breakfast bar, and Mrs. Dobbs was cutting him off a slice of red velvet cake. He looked at his watch in a way that suggested he'd been there since egg salad sandwiches.

We crouched down below the window and spoke in whispers. "How could he find us so quick like that?" I said.

"They have ways," Justine said mysteriously.

Bobby Ray looked most scared of all. "My inhaler," he whispered.

"What inhaler?" I said. I'd never seen him use an inhaler. He'd been too busy washing his hands all the time.

"I carry one just in case," he said.

"In case of what?"

"In case I should catch asthma. Spontaneously."

Justine was as confused as I was. "Spontaneously catch asthma?" she asked in a voice a shade meaner than she probably meant it to sound.

"I don't think asthma is something you can just catch," I explained, as if Bobby Ray didn't speak girl.

"I know that, but I worry about a lot of things," Bobby Ray snapped back. I knew that was true. I snuck a look up at Ed and Mrs. Dobbs. Sure enough, there on the breakfast bar was a kid inhaler. I could see that it had a prescription label taped around it. Ed didn't exactly have to be Sherlock Holmes to track us.

I ducked back down and snapped at Bobby Ray, "You didn't notice you lost it?"

He shrugged. "I never use it."

There was a silver lining there, though. Faced with Ed Hemet taking away our claim on history, suddenly Bobby Ray was on our side. Maybe Oprah had finally reached him, too. If he was still worried about violating the sci-fi prime directive, he wasn't saying.

Schooley/McCorkle

We'd have to get in and get that disc out of his room before the Ed Hemet people made it disappear. The front door and the stairs were out of the kitchen's line of sight, so if we were ninja about it, we could sneak in and get that disc and get it out of there.

We went back around to the front of the house, and I slowly turned the handle, and pulled the door open just enough to slip in. We padded like cats through the front hall. It was a good thing it was a new house, because one squeaky floorboard could have given us up. It was all going according to plan, when Bobby Ray had to walk past the bathroom at the bottom of the stairs.

He stopped as if the vanity sink had a magnetic pull on him. It was obvious that the sink was his first stop whenever he got home. I wanted to scream in his ear, "Your hands ain't dirty, Bobby Ray! Snap out of it!"

But that was obviously not an option available to a would-be ninja. So I did the next best thing. I started yanking on his earlobe, figuring pain was a good motivator in situations like that. Not that I could that Bobby Ray's momma didn't really know any details about me or Justine, and we hadn't dropped any prescription medication at the scene, so maybe Ed would just focus his search in Shady Brook. My house would be safe.

Schooley/McCorkle

honestly say I had ever faced a situation quite like that. Who had? But I had limited options, and Bobby Ray seemed hypnotized by that big pump bottle of liquid soap. It was only when we heard Ed Hemet's voice volume increasing that Bobby Ray broke free and followed us up the steps. Even running from disaster he had to give his doorknob three turns.

We slipped into Bobby Ray's room, and I kept the door cracked to keep watch. As Bobby Ray went to his computer, I could see Mrs. Dobbs walking Ed to the door. He handed her a card, and she assured him that she'd call when her boy got home. I thought we were home free. Then Bobby Ray pushed the eject button on his disc drive. This woke his computer out of hibernation, which would have been fine, except he had mail. On Bobby Ray's computer a new e-mail is announced not by the "You've got mail" guy but by a cheesy version of the theme from *Star Wars* blaring from his speakers. Maybe if he'd just had the tiny little computer speakers like most of the world, this wouldn't have been a problem, but Bobby Ray had a subwoofer that shook the room. I could see Ed look

Schooley/McCorkle

up the stairs in the split second before I shut the door.

"He's coming up here!" I screamed, but in a whisper.

Bobby Ray went to his windowsill and pulled something out. There are times when being worried about everything can actually pay off, and this was one of those times. Bobby Ray's window was outfitted with a rope ladder fire escape that he dropped to reach the ground. He had never climbed down it, seeing as his house had never been on fire, and he was afraid of heights. If I'd had a cool ladder that I could go in and out of my bedroom window with, I would have never used the front door. But that's just me.

I stuffed the CD into my pants. Justine went down the ladder first. Bobby Ray froze, but when he saw me coming at his earlobe, he fell in line. As I stepped out the window, I heard a knock at the bedroom door and Mrs. Dobbs calling Bobby Ray. I dipped just below their view as the door opened.

I considered that we should let the air out of Ed Hemet's tires to give us a head start, but then I figured that Bobby Ray's momma didn't really know any details about me or Justine, and we hadn't dropped any prescription medication at the scene, so maybe Ed would just focus his search in Shady Brook. My house would be safe.

Chapter THIRTEEN

It felt like we ran for ten minutes before anybody had the nerve to stop and look back to see if the Feds were on to us. Strangely, it was Bobby Ray who stopped first. That may have had more to do with him being out of breath than being brave, though. No sign of Ed Hemet.

"Maybe he just wanted to return the inhaler," Justine wishfully thought out loud. I don't think even she believed it, but she wanted to.

"Maybe," I said.

"Yeah, maybe," Bobby Ray added pointlessly. The way he was wheezing and spitting in the dirt, it was surely an ironic time to be inhaler-less.

In our hearts we all knew Ed would catch up

sooner or later, and that only made us more anxious to get to my house and start reading the future. It was too bad that we couldn't see the future right then, though, because we would have seen that a train was coming.

The train crossing was in sight when we heard the whistle blow. I tried to pick up the pace, but Bobby Ray just couldn't, and Justine wouldn't leave him behind. Admirable, I suppose, but I had the CD on me, and I figured Bobby Ray was already a wanted man anyway. For the sake of Justine's twisted sense of loyalty, I tried to keep formation, but that train was coming up fast. You didn't have to be Einstein or even Tom Cruise to see the train was going to beat us to that crossing. We kept going anyway, I guess because no one wanted to sound like a quitter.

The crossing lights started flashing. Bobby Ray must have opened up his adrenaline reserves, because he suddenly got in gear and shot out in front of us. Unconsciously, it slowed me and Justine down, trying to make sense of the miracle. It was like he was some kind of crazy John Henry, determined to

Schooley/McCorkle

beat that machine. For a minute I thought he might do it too. I thought about hurling the CD in the air for him to relay over the tracks to the finish line. It would have been magnificent, if only Bobby Ray hadn't tripped on an old hubcap and landed facedown in the dirt, inches away from the thundering locomotive.

Now we were stuck on the Ed Hemet side of town. At least Bobby Ray had something to keep his mind off it, since he was taking a full wetnap bath after his spill. The train seemed like an endless line of boxcars and tankers. In the road a few cars pulled to a stop at the crossing. I went from watching for the end of the train to watching for Ed Hemet's car to join the line.

Four cars were backed up when Ed Hemet's became the fifth.

"Uh-oh," we all said at the same time. Any of us could have shouted, "Jinx, you owe me a Coke," at that moment, and been owed two Cokes. It just wasn't the time or place, not with a freight train on one side of us and a G-man on the other. The scrap yard was on the wrong side of the tracks, so even trying to hide in a junked truck wasn't an option. Making a lateral move wouldn't have helped any because of the way the road curved; Ed would have spotted us as soon as we'd walked away from the line of cars. The train kept rolling. I had an idea.

I tapped on the window of the first car by the crossing. It was a big Cadillac, about twenty years old and pink, except for the rusty parts. It was not all that unusual a vehicle for Kudzu, but I did not recognize this particular driver. It was an old lady behind the wheel, leaning so far forward her nose practically touched the windshield. She had frizzed-out hair of a color that could only have come out of a bottle labeled RONALD MCDONALD. Contrasting with the orange were blue eyes. I mean, technically she had brown eyes, I guess, but there was so much makeup around them that the predominant effect was blue. She was either hypnotized or deafened by the train, because she didn't respond to my window tap. I had to pound.

I think I might have scared her. She jerked back from the window and turned to us with a hair-raising scream. That scared me right back. But I had no choice but to carry on with my evolving plan.

"Ma'am," I said, "my brother here is real sick and needs to get home right away. If you wouldn't mind, could we hop a ride?" I'm not sure that Bobby Ray was exactly born to play the role of my brother, but he looked plenty enough sick for this story.

Justine smiled, which helped.

The lady looked us up and down and said, "He's not going to puke, is he?" She wasn't what you would call the grandmotherly type. Probably lived with a lot of cats, I figured. Just as I was thinking that, I noticed that she actually had a cat in a carrier on the bench seat beside her. I'm a good judge of people.

The end of the train was closing in. If we didn't get in that car, the line of traffic would start moving and Ed would no doubt round that curve and see us running.

Time almost out, I promised the cranky old lady that the sickness in question wasn't messy or contagious. She let out a put-upon sigh and hit the electric door locks. We piled into the backseat just as the track cleared, Bobby Ray wheezing, either acting or for real. There was a lot of cat fur in that car.

We slumped down on the big white leather seat. I mean, it was white at some point, but right then it was kind of brownish. I talked her to my house by a roundabout way, just in case we were being followed. Justine saw Ed turn off for the highway, and we all relaxed. Except the driver, that is. She kind of had an episode when she glanced in the rearview and saw Bobby Ray wiping down her leather seat with a wet-nap. That spot did look cleaner, but she didn't appreciate the gesture and kicked us to the curb right then and there.

Mission accomplished anyway, because we'd ditched Ed Hemet and were only a block or so from home, safe home.

Chapter FOURTEEN

We had a family computer, but it wasn't as fancy as Bobby Ray's. Then again, it wouldn't blast the theme from *Star Wars* at an inopportune moment, so that was a plus.

Momma was out, so we could proceed without risk. I put the disc in and prayed that it was compatible with our outdated Windows. All I got was a little *bloop* and a message that said there was some kind of "critical runtime error." I hated that message. It wasn't as though I'd stuck a slice of cheese in the drawer. What could have been so critical?

Bobby Ray knew exactly what was wrong, he said. So I got up to let him have at it. But he just stood there and stared at my keyboard.

"What's wrong, Bobby Ray?" Justine said with more compassion in her voice than I thought Bobby Ray deserved.

I suddenly remembered the disinfectant spray next to Bobby Ray's computer. This inspired me to look at my keyboard through Bobby Ray's eyes. There was peanut butter residue on the space bar. Some Fritos crumbs in the gaps between the keys. A greasy shine from the Fritos on the keys themselves. A couple of sticky spots of Coke. But I wouldn't call it disgusting.

Bobby Ray stared at it like it harbored the black plague itself.

I made a mental note that I would try to cure Bobby Ray of his debilities before the summer was out. Then I went and got some Formula 409, knowing that wasn't his usual brand but hoping it would do. When I was done, those keys were so clean that I'd almost rubbed the letters off. Satisfied, Bobby Ray sat down, and in about half a minute he'd fixed the problem.

Justine and me were almost cheek to cheek as we

crowded in to read the screen. But then Bobby Ray's big old sweaty head pushed between us and killed the mood.

We skimmed through the pages quickly, just looking at the big headlines. Ordinarily the local summer newspaper was used for protecting the driveway from spray paint, and not much else. When school was back in session, I'd have to start concocting current event reports out of the *Democrat-Star-Leader*, which is the name of the Kudzu newspaper. I'd always wondered about that name; it was so long for such a skinny paper.

I didn't know if the *New York Times* was always so dull, but based on what little I'd seen up to that point, it looked like it was going to be a boring summer. My folks' pick for president of the United States seemed to go from bad to worse in the polls, but I didn't need a CD from the future to tell me that their guy would be a big loser in the fall. As a rule Momma and Daddy liked losers. Apparently the candidate was done in by a scandal that some reporter named "Hogstrogate," which made absolutely no sense to me.

The Olympics would go on, and the USA would win more than anybody, but again, this was to be expected. It wasn't until Bobby Ray skipped to August twentieth that anything of local interest caught our notice, and we almost missed that one because we all realized that that would be the first day of school, which meant all of the headlines from there on out would be potential current event clippings. Assuming any of the stories would make it into the *Democrat-Star-Leader*. At a glance, I'd say most of them probably wouldn't.

There was a drawing of a cow and a headline that said, BELOVED CHILDREN'S AUTHOR C. C. LEE DIES. But it was the cow that caught my eye. It was Miss Moo from the book *A Farm for All Seasons*. Kids everywhere had to read that book in third grade, but kids in Kudzu were required to like it. This was because the man who wrote it lived down the way from the college, and he was probably the most famous thing for a hundred miles. Every year some poor sap third grader had to dress like Miss Moo and get his picture put in the paper, which would only be the beginning of that person's troubles once that paper became fair game for cutting up. A teacher told me that old C. C. himself showed up at one of these book parties once when she was a kid in our school. That our teacher had once sat at the small desks was weird enough, but to imagine that the guy on the back of *A Farm for All Seasons* had ever sat at a teacher's desk, that was plain inconceivable.

And now he was dead.

Justine, with her instinct to go for the bright side first, said, "He still has the whole summer."

"Technically, since summer isn't really over until September twenty-first, C. C. Lee will miss a full month of it," Bobby Ray corrected.

"So will we because we'll be back in school," I said, trying to put this all into meaningful perspective. School wasn't as bad as being dead, maybe, but it wasn't as good as vacation.

Bobby Ray grimly added, "He has eighty-seven days left," doing the math in his head instantly and silently, like he always did.

Justine got a sick look about her, "Well, we have

to warn him." She stood, and we still sat, not quite getting her drift. She waved her arms some, as if that might create an updraft to get us up off our butts.

"Wouldn't you want to know if you had only eighty-seven days left to live?" Justine flapped.

Bobby Ray had to go wash his hands. Clearly this whole thing was creeping him out. I considered Justine's question. Would I want to know? I wasn't sure. I thought about the army bride on the van again. I guess everyone wants to know everything that will play on them personally, but knowing that you had only eighty-seven days left to live might just qualify as too much information. Not to mention being the one doing the telling of something like that; it didn't seem polite.

By the time Bobby Ray had come back, flicking his pink and wrinkly hands through the air to dry them, Justine's mind was made up. This meant that ours were too, whether we liked it or not. Justine didn't know the way to C. C. Lee's house, but I did. You had to live in Kudzu a long time to know. Tourists would come through town every so often with beat-up old copies of Miss Moo's adventures on their dashboards, looking to meet the man. But the folks in town would never tell them how to find the house they were looking for, even if they were standing in front of it. Usually we'd get them so lost with made-up directions that they'd turn back to the city as soon as they could find a highway. It was something to do.

We grabbed one of Momma's pies. I figured that if someone came to tell me I was about to die, if that someone also brought along a good pie, that might soften the blow, or at least provide a change of subject. It was strawberry rhubarb, which wouldn't have been in my top ten favorites, but I figured it'd be good for someone old like C. C. Lee.

Pie in hand, we hiked over to C. C.'s house. Justine frequently took the lead even though she was the one who didn't know where she was going.

The house was big and old, like you'd expect. There was a tall fence and a deep front yard, and giant oaks that kept the house in shadows. The wrought-iron gate wasn't locked or anything, so in reality any tourist who knew what was what could have done what we were about to do.

Bobby Ray was having third thoughts about our whole enterprise, but Justine shoved him forward and he fell against the gate hard enough that it swung open wide. Pushed forward by a grim sense of duty, we crunched up the gravel driveway to the pillars on the front porch. My eyes adjusted to the shade, and I took a good look at the house. It was probably a hundred, hundred fifty years old, and it looked more like a funeral home than the actual funeral home on Main Street. That seemed about right to me, considering an about-to-be-dead man was living in it. We got to the door, which was criss-crossed with fancy glass squares. I tried to get a look inside, but it was just a dark hall giving up no clues as to what was really going on in there. I rang the bell. After a minute, Justine tried too. We looked at our feet, all probably thinking the same thing.

I said it out loud, "What if old C. C. has already expired, and nobody was gonna find him until the day before that newspaper story? Stuff like that happens." I thought Bobby Ray would just pass out right there. Evidently he had not been thinking that. What he *had* been thinking, probably, was that we should just go home and wash our hands. Justine wasn't going anywhere. She rattled the doorknob, which was locked. This was not normal for Kudzu, but I suspected that this was more about trying to keep out northern tourists than trying to keep out local ax murderers.

I noticed some empty oxygen tanks on the porch, arranged like someone was going to maybe swap them for full ones. I felt like I was Sherlock Holmes, except I already knew the end to the mystery and I was still collecting clues anyway.

Bobby Ray would have been happy to leave the pie on the porch with a note, and run. Justine, and to a lesser degree, me, thought that it was improper to just leave a note telling someone when they were going to die. We had to make every effort to deliver the message in person.

Not far from the door, a calico cat jumped out an open window, giving all of us a start. Justine looked at the lace curtain drifting in the breeze, and I knew what she was thinking.

The job of climbing up the trellis and in that open

window would fall to me. There was never a question that Bobby Ray would do such a thing, and I didn't want Justine to think for a minute that I wasn't noble. When I flopped onto the wood floor of the room, it made more of a racket than I'd expected. Maybe it was just in relation to how quiet the house was. Other than a clock ticking somewhere, C. C. Lee's house might have been the quietest place I'd ever heard. There weren't any lights on, but I could smell that I was surrounded by books. My eyes adjusted to the dim light, and I could see the room was his study, stuffed with maybe four times the books in my folks' collection. On the desk there was one small Miss Moo drawing in a frame, and that was the only sign of that dumb cow.

Trying not to make any further commotion, I went over to the front hall and let in Justine and Bobby Ray. She marched right in; he hesitated, of course, but followed. We tiptoed around the writer's silent house like we were in a museum and we didn't want the guard to yell at us. Finally, when we got all the way to the back, we found him.

The world-famous C. C. Lee was in a giant leather

chair that made him look small. His feet were propped on an embroidered hassock, and there was a heavy Indian blanket tucked all around him. His face was gray and sunk in, with a tube going from his nose to one of those tanks on a wheeled cart behind him. He stared out a picture window to his backyard garden. A squirrel was out there, running in circles. He didn't seem to notice that we were even in his room. It was all so still and spooky that I thought Bobby Ray was going to need that oxygen himself.

For a second I thought my premonition that C. C. Lee was already deceased was true, but then he blinked and slowly looked away from the crazy squirrel and directly at us. His eyes were yellow and watery. He didn't look famous; he looked like he was going to die.

I grabbed the pie from Bobby Ray.

"Y'all like strawberry rhubarb, Mr. C. C.?" I heard myself saying to him. He stared at us with a puzzled look for what felt like ten years, then he called me Johnny. Now, I didn't claim that I was Johnny, but at the same time I didn't claim that I wasn't. It just seemed like a prudent flexibility to not commit, considering that we had just busted into this man's house.

Mr. C. C. talked some more to me, but it didn't make much sense. Kept saying I was a good boy and stuff. Not that I wasn't, basically, but how would he know? He asked me to fetch the paper, the mention of which snapped me back to our mission. But as I tried to find the words, Justine noticed something that put this whole Johnny business into an unexpected perspective. Above the fireplace there was a nice, big oil painting of a much younger C. C. with a handsome woman, and between them was a big Labrador retriever. On the dog's collar a name was stitched: Johnny.

The situation was this: The most famous man in Kudzu thought that I was his dead dog.

Schooley/McCorkle

Chapter FIFTEEN

Nobody wanted to leap right in there and break the news to C. C. that I wasn't his dog, so I slipped away and went looking for the kitchen to find pie plates and silverware. I couldn't find a proper pie knife, and I wished I had brought one. Momma had plenty. I did the best I could with a steak knife and a spatula, getting a piece onto the plate and trying to sculpt it back into a pie-slice shape after the fact.

When I got back with the pie, Bobby Ray was standing in the corner, but Justine had pulled up a chair to talk with the old man. Somehow he knew that she wasn't a dog, but even though I handed him a plate of pie in such a way that my opposable thumb was in full view, he still called me Johnny.

I'd called the strawberry rhubarb right, because he cleaned his plate. Justine was running out of soothing chitchat, and I sensed that it was time to tell him the bad news about his eighty-seven remaining days. I wondered if he'd believe me, not for the usual Liar reasons but for the Johnny reason. But before I could do it, he turned to Bobby Ray, who was trying to meld with the plaster wall, and told him, "You best take Johnny out so he can do his business."

Bobby Ray froze, not sure what to do, but Justine, without missing a beat, said to him, "Go on, Bobby Ray. Take Johnny out for a walk."

That's how we ended up in the backyard, me on my hands and knees, watching through the picture window as Justine broke the news to C. C. Lee. It was a sight to see. Justine looked so sweet and nice, leaning forward to put her perfect young hand on his old shriveled and spotted one. Even though we'd been in the yard long enough for a dog to water the plants and drop some biscuits, we stayed outside. It's not that we were chicken or anything, it just looked like Justine was doing such a cracking good job. She looked like

Schooley/McCorkle

an angel. Of *death*, in this case, but an angel just the same. She even managed to make the doomed guy smile. I couldn't imagine how she'd managed that.

Justine got up suddenly, and C. C. turned and stared out the window, now at us instead of at the crazy squirrel. For some reason I pretended to lift my leg. It was the least I could do.

That is when Justine came out into the yard. I felt more than ridiculous, but she didn't even comment on it. She just quietly said, "Let's go now."

Walking back through town, nobody said anything for two or three blocks. We just went slow and didn't look at each other.

Finally I had to ask, "So what did he say when you told him?"

Justine finally looked up at me and said, "I didn't."

"Didn't what?" I said.

"Tell him," Justine said. "I asked him what he thought it would be like if you could tell the future and know everything that was going to happen to you. He said that he didn't think that he would care for it much at all, because if you spent your time worrying about what was going to happen tomorrow, then you couldn't really savor today."

"He was watching a squirrel!" I said. "You call that savoring?"

Justine just sighed and said that she thought that C. C. knew his days were numbered. When it came down to it, she just didn't see the use in telling him the exact number. She said that while I was pretending to pee on his camellias, he told her a story about how he went to see a fortune-teller when he was a young man.

"This fortune-teller," C. C. told Justine, "she predicted that I would become a famous author. So I spent years trying to write big, important novels. Nothing happened, and I just thought that the old woman was a charlatan. But a funny thing happened when I stopped worrying about her prediction. I wrote a little children's book. Just for fun."

"Miss Moo!" Bobby Ray shouted out like he was on a game show called *No Duh*.

I rolled my eyes at Bobby Ray, then turned back to Justine, trying to figure out if there was a kidding-akidder thing happening. "Man, he sure opened up after we left the room," I said, attempting to arch an eyebrow. Probably came off as a nervous twitch, though, because Justine didn't pick up on it.

It's interesting to know where you're going, but it's more interesting how you get there, was the point to his fortune-teller story, Justine said.

If I hadn't been falling hard for Justine, I would have been kind of ticked that she'd chickened out, seeing as she was the one who had made us all go over there in the first place. Bobby Ray asked her what she'd said to the old man to make him smile.

"Nothing," Justine said. "It's what he said to me."

"So what'd he say?"

She laughed, and told us what he'd said: "Why is that boy down on all fours?"

I'm still not sure if C. C. Lee was yanking my chain or Justine was. Could be both of them were. One thing was for sure, the expression "dog days of summer" would now have a personal meaning for me.

Chapter SIXTEEN

It was almost supper time when we got back from our mercy mission. Momma was cooking something with bulgur wheat and walnuts that she called Cheat Loaf. She was always coming up with cutesy names for her creations, as if that somehow made them more edible. It was not really an invite-people-over kind of meal, but she did anyway. As much as I wanted Justine to stay and Bobby Ray to go, the opposite happened. Her Daddy pulled up in his Be-All-You-Can-Be mobile just as we were sitting down. Truthfully, I think from the first whiff of the steaming Cheat Loaf, Justine was looking for an exit strategy. She could have asked her daddy in for some, but even Momma knew that the Army didn't march on a belly full of bulgur.

Justine did invite me over to eat on the base with her and her folks, so I didn't take her speedy exit personally. I knew it was about Momma's cooking, not me.

The unforeseen thing was that Bobby Ray seemed eager to tie on the vegan feed bag. It was like he'd discovered yet another way to be weird. Or maybe it was Momma's little talk about the dangers of E. coli and salmonella and filthy factory farming that made Bobby Ray want to eat some meatless meat. Either way, before I could do anything about it, Bobby Ray was at our supper table.

Daddy was never particularly comfortable at small talk with strangers, and Bobby Ray was nothing if not strange. I kind of regretted the story I'd made up at the college about Bobby Ray, since it seemed to make Daddy extra uncomfortable at the table. He talked slowly to him as if entertaining an exchange student from Bulgaria. I think Bobby Ray probably concluded my daddy was an idiot. I sure would have if I hadn't known that he was thinking a similar idea about Bobby Ray.

In one of the silences during the meal, Bobby Ray started tapping his fork three times against his plate before stabbing each piece of Cheat Loaf. It was distracting. Finally, in an attempt to talk away the tapping, Momma asked Bobby Ray how he liked his food. The answer was pretty obvious, I thought, since he was eating a lot more than anyone else at the table. The talk about nothing ran out pretty fast, so the regular *tap-tap-tap*, chew-chew-chew sounds coming from Bobby Ray started working on all our nerves. Momma was probably heavily regretting her polite invite, but she smiled anyway and tried to act like he was normal.

Daddy asked, "So how'd the tutoring go up at the college today?" I had to jump on that question like it was a live grenade. I couldn't give Bobby Ray time to think, much less speak.

"What—" was all he got out before I talked over him.

"Turns out Bobby Ray had a lot to teach *me*, Daddy," I said, winking with the eye that Bobby Ray couldn't see. Daddy gave me a meaningful wink back like he was fixing to nominate me for sainthood.

Schooley/McCorkle

Bobby Ray was tapping and chewing, and I knew I had until he swallowed to bail out. I hid some pepper in my hand and sniffed. When the sneeze came, I took aim at Bobby Ray's tapping hand. Got it good, too. Anything he meant to say was instantly forgotten. He sprung from the table like some kind of germ-fearing jackrabbit.

While he was in the bathroom, no doubt scrubbing off a layer of skin, I quickly finished my supper and cleared out of the dining room. When I peeked behind me, I could see Momma and Daddy already running to the child psychology section of their library. Pondering the many sick sides of Bobby Ray would keep them out of my hair for the rest of the night.

I met Bobby Ray outside the bathroom door and told him supper was over.

"But I'm not finished eating," he moaned.

"Momma and Daddy run a tight ship," I lied. I had a milk crate packed with snacks in my closet; he wouldn't starve.

The future was on our computer, and I wanted to see some good stuff. The only problem was that the computer was in the family room and was usually used by me to play Doom. I was pretty sure that looking at the front pages of the *New York Times* would not look like Doom, at least at a glance. So I needed a cover story.

I whispered to Momma and Daddy that I was going to help Bobby Ray learn to use the computer. Daddy gave me a proud thumbs-up. I thought if I could sustain this little lie a while longer, when Daddy eventually found out that Bobby Ray was a genius, I might have set the stage to take credit for it.

The first thing I looked for was a story about the Vespucci probe crashing. I figured that somebody might have leaked what had happened at some point, and blown the lid off of Ed Hemet's cover-up. There was nothing. Then I had a scarier notion. I scanned through for a story about three kids from a tiny town that no one had ever heard of until these kids had mysteriously disappeared simultaneously. I didn't say this one to Bobby Ray, because if we did come across a story like that, I didn't want him peeing himself in our nice office chair.

There were no mysterious disappearances, or unsolved triple homicides, or any incidents that would lead me to think anything other than that Ed Hemet would leave us alone. His scientists would no doubt conclude that the disc had burned up on reentry. At least that's the story I told myself so I wouldn't feel like a wanted man all summer long. Urgent matters done, I started reading for fun.

The thing about reading the front page of the *New York Times* is that—at least from the experience of this Kudzu boy—even if you are reading about the future, it's honestly no more interesting than reading about the past or the present. Other famous people passed, but once we got past C. C. Lee's sad fate, it wasn't anybody that meant anything to me.

Bobby Ray read along, close over my shoulder, breathing just loud and annoying enough to make me drift back to topics of homicide. I suggested that we take turns reading, me first. He eased back onto Momma's settee and proceeded to ramble on about the amazing things he's found on eBay. "Amazing" being a flexible word, in this case. I quickly realized I was in better shape with the wheezing.

While I discovered that we were in for a record heat wave in the South, followed by a week of rain, Bobby Ray bragged about his collection of mint in-the-box *Star Wars* toys. I got the feeling he didn't get to talk to anyone about his personal fixations very much. At least not to anyone who cared. Truthfully, this streak went unbroken, even though I nodded like I was listening. Then he started asking me questions, and I was forced to actually pay some attention to his quest for a vintage Tusken Raider. Reading the *New York Times* and listening to a boy genius talk about his toys at the same time was putting my multitasking skills to a test that I was flunking. If anything important happened between July twenty-fifth and August third, chances are I missed it, thanks to Bobby Ray's gum flapping. When he started in on his mislabeled carbonite Han Solo, I turned over the reading chores, hoping that it might have the effect of shutting his pie hole.

At the computer Bobby Ray did seem to zone out a little. Maybe because I wasn't distracting him the way

Schooley/McCorkle

he had been distracting me. Or maybe the computer was his happy place and he wasn't used to company when it was just the man and his machine. Either way was good by me. While I observed from a respectful distance, Bobby Ray zoomed through pages with his advanced-placement reading skills. Before I could even properly fluff up the settee cushion that Bobby Ray had pancaked, he'd hit the end of the summer and the end of the news of the future. Bobby Ray concluded that they must have cut it off there because they'd had to make the CD and install it on the probe. The only conclusion I could make was that the summer would continue the long tradition of nothing happening in Kudzu.

Not that I expected a big juicy Kudzu scandal on the front page of the *New York Times*. I had been hoping for a headline about something truly amazing, like shooting bigfoot, or Jesus coming back. Something that was worthy of Oprah's interest. Predicting rain seemed unlikely to turn the trick.

It was a fact that we hadn't exactly read every word, but I was getting tired of breathing in the fog of

Formula 409 that Bobby Ray continued to spew on the family computer, so I yawned loud and wide, declared the future a waste, and suggested, "Your momma's probably wondering whether you're dead or alive, Bobby Ray."

"I sent her an I.M. from here; she knows," Bobby Ray said, not getting the hint. "I I.M. her from my room all the time," he added, as if that were a normal thing to do. Bobby Ray may be the only kid in the world who I.M.'s his own mother. From inside his own house.

Bobby Ray may have gotten an A+ in social studies, but he was failing in social skills. Seeing that my subtle approach wasn't getting the results I was looking for, I went for direct.

"Okay, Bobby Ray, we've been together all day and I need a little *me* time," I said, borrowing one of Momma's favorite expressions. He got the hint, once I stopped hinting and started saying.

Daddy gave Bobby Ray a ride home and I went along, just to be sure that Bobby Ray didn't say anything smart. After we dropped him off, Daddy told me

Schooley/McCorkle

he was proud of me for trying to help Bobby Ray get along. It was probably a good time to set the record straight about Bobby Ray and his sky-high IQ, but I didn't. I accepted Daddy's compliment because I figured just hanging around with Bobby Ray Dobbs from morning to night was above and beyond what any other kid in Kudzu had ever done.

When we got home, Momma was sitting on the front porch with a sweaty glass of ice water and a big child psychology book. She put a bookmark in when we came up, but I knew she was digging into Bobby Ray's peculiarities. I think it made her happy to have a new test subject. Daddy went into the kitchen and dished up some homemade vanilla ice cream. As trying as Momma's main courses could be, her desserts almost made up for it. She even made hot fudge from scratch, mixing up cream and sugar and Nestlé's semisweet chocolate chips. Momma said it would be better with some French-sounding chocolate, but she knew better than to go looking in Kudzu for stuff imported from Europe.

The three of us sat on the porch and ate our

sundaes. I creaked back and forth on the porch swing; they sat on the steps, whispering to each other. No doubt about Bobby Ray. But then Momma came up next to me on the swing and started asking about Justine.

The humid night air instantly felt that much hotter. The sound of the crickets caught my ear. I tried to change the subject, but my first reaction to her must have given me away. It was my chance to come clean. I could tell them about the space probe, about the future, about C. C. Lee, about Oprah, about the kiss in the giant heart. I could just start laying out the truth and go all night long.

"She's okay. Kind of bossy," I said, hoping to leave it at that.

Daddy stood up next to us and said, "Pretty, though."

"I guess. Didn't really notice," I answered, even though it was barely a question. I dipped my spoon in my dish and held it as high as I could to let the fudge run off into my mouth. It was something I used to do when I was little, and I hoped if I started acting immature, they would relax and call off the interrogation.

It worked, kind of. They stopped asking questions, all right. But instead they stared at me and swapped gooey looks with each other. I would rather have kept going on the questions. At least then I could have fought back.

I went to bed. It had been a long day.

Chapter SEVENTEEN

The next morning was a Friday. I ate my breakfast in front of the computer reading Saturday's news. When I was trying to get to sleep, this thought occurred to me: If I just read the news in depth a day ahead all summer, I could still dip my toe in the future, without boring myself to sleep by trying to read it all in one sitting. Alas, even reading all of the little stories didn't uncover anything that seemed worth knowing. Politicians had rallies in Ohio. The mayor of New York gave an important speech about something. Congress was on recess. I pictured people in suits on monkey bars. Man, now that would have been a good front page picture. No such luck, so I kept reading.

Our dollar fell against Japan's yen, whatever that

meant. Bobby Ray or Daddy would probably know. And I still wouldn't care.

I hung around the house, half expecting Justine would just spontaneously show up. She didn't. I thought that maybe it had been more than Momma's crazy entrée that had driven her out the night before. What if it had been me? I moped around all morning, thinking the situation over.

Finally I decided that I had kept my feelings for Justine bottled up for too long. I had to tell someone. I told Momma I was going out to play, and I walked into town. This called for an expert opinion.

Tommy Doolittle could usually be found in front of Jackson's store sucking on a bottle of Dr Pepper and giving advice for free. His name was excellently appropriate, because he really did do very little as far as anyone could tell. Even better would have been Tommy Do-nothing, I guess, but I don't think that Do-nothing is a real name.

He leaned against the wall with one leg kicked up behind to brace himself. Even though he was as old as my daddy, he looked cool in that pose. Not that he leaned like that to look good. He told me his story the first time I stopped by Jackson's after school. Tommy said that he'd mashed his spine when a whole pallet of fifty-pound bags of fertilizer fell on him at Garden Depot. Ever since then he'd been getting a fat monthly check from Garden Depot world headquarters in Atlanta. The downside to all this was that he couldn't bend over or sit down anymore. I'm not sure if all that was true, but I hadn't made it up, so I assumed it was. One thing was for sure: I thought of Tommy whenever we went to Garden Depot. And I avoided the fertilizer aisle entirely.

Tommy took to reading romance novels from the rack at Jackson's while he stood out in front. Not buying them, just reading them and putting them back. I asked him once why he didn't go to the college library, but he just said, "Too many chairs, boy." Nobody seemed to mind him there at Jackson's anyway. For us kids it was like having a living cigar store Indian. His skin actually looked like carved wood, from standing out in the elements day after day. I think Mrs. Jackson liked having a man around, since she took over the store all by herself. Not that Tommy Doolittle was in the physical shape to stop a robbery, but the chances of a robbery were pretty slim anyway.

Sometimes on my way home from school, I'd hang there and drink a bottle of Dr Pepper with Tommy and talk about stupid stuff. But that Friday, I was going to Tommy for what he knew best: romance.

Tommy could quote whole speeches from *Love's Savage Spectacle* or *Passionate Glances*. He may have looked like leather, but he had a poet's heart. I once suggested to Daddy that he and Tommy had a lot in common that way, but Daddy didn't seem to agree. Daddy said that Tommy was full of that which had fallen on him at Garden Depot. But Daddy didn't ever stop to really listen to Tommy like I did.

When I got to Jackson's, Tommy was there leaning, as always. I went in and bought a couple of Dr Pepper's, giving him one as a goodwill gesture for his consulting services.

"So you got girl problems?" Tommy asked between swigs.

"Yeah," I said. "I think she likes me okay as a

friend, but I'm not sure she thinks of me in a boyfriend-type way."

Tommy leafed through the paperback he was reading, *Heart of Desire*, looking for a helpful nugget of advice. Finally he found something.

He read in his low gravelly way, "She whispered into the nape of his neck that she was his, she'd always been his. He quivered in anticipation of her one true kiss."

Tommy shut the book up and looked at me as if he had just imparted the wisdom of Romeo. I didn't get it, but I couldn't admit it to Tommy, as I didn't want to seem romantically thickheaded. It was difficult to foresee circumstances that would involve Justine whispering into the nape of my neck, that was for sure. It was frustrating to know the future of things I didn't care about, yet not have a clue about where this Justine deal was going.

"Do you think I should try whispering in her neck nape?" I asked.

"Don't work that way, boy," Tommy said, and

shook his head. "First you and your lady have to sur-vive some high adventure together."

Space probe crash. Check.

"Then," Tommy continued, "she has to marry a cruel, merciless man . . . who you try to kill."

He was losing me.

"You are sentenced to hard time at a remote penal colony for the deed," Tommy said in a matter-of-fact tone that didn't square in my mind with the words "penal colony." I didn't exactly have a frame of ref-erence for this phrase, but I did not like the sound of it. There was no stopping Tommy, though. "Once on this blistering island or freezing mountain top, you will nearly waste away from the squalid, sick condi-tions. After years of tortured separation, if she still desires you, she'll find you and nurse you back to hale and hearty and into her loving arms. That's real love as I see it, boy."

Maybe Daddy had been right about Tommy after all.

I stared out at the road and finished up my Dr Pepper. Seemed like a lot of trouble for a couple of twelve-year-olds to go through.

Before I could ponder the usefulness of Tommy's advice too deeply, an odd sight on Main Street caught my eye. Three identical Ford Explorers pulled to a stop in front of the Mason Jar Café. The fact that it was three matching vehicles was plenty unusual; add in the detail that they were all clean and shiny, and it might as well have been Elvis coming to town. Weddings, funerals, and July Fourth parades were about the only occasions on which you'd come across three clean cars in a row in Kudzu. In my gut I knew what those spotless Fords meant.

Chapter EIGHTEEN

Ed Hemet was back.

Or maybe he'd never left. It was hard to say. He could have been holed up at one of the new motels out by exit 76, off Highway 2. Nobody from town ever went nosing around out there unless they were looking for trouble, Momma always said. What sort of trouble was never made clear to me, but I took her at her word, because unlike me, Momma wasn't a liar.

Ed and five other guys dressed in Ed-wear piled out of their big government rides and into the Mason Jar Café. I figured if they were staying out on the highway, maybe they'd gotten sick of Bob Evans and the Hometown Buffet. The neon sign in the window of the Mason Jar couldn't have hurt either:

INE
OOD
OR
INER
OLKS

I assumed that, being government operatives, they would have deduced that there was supposed to be a giant F that stretched in front of all those words so the sign made sense. That F had been missing for as long as I could remember. Growing up, I'd just assumed the sign was written in Swedish. Only when they changed their menus and added "Fine Food for Finer Folks" on the front did I realize that it had been an American restaurant all along. Why they'd spent their money on new menus before fixing a busted sign, I could never figure out. Kudzu was full of little mysteries like that.

When I snuck a peek inside, I saw that the Mason Jar was empty except for One-Eyed Jack in the cowboy

Schooley/McCorkle

hat, who always sat at the counter with a cup of milky coffee and a crossword puzzle book. He could be found on that particular stool about as reliably as Tommy Doolittle could be spotted at his post. Once they'd both witnessed a fender bender on Main Street, but One-Eyed Jack's testimony was thrown out because of his depth perception limitations.

Ed walked with the others past Jack to the last of the empty booths. They obviously didn't want prying ears. Not that they would have had a problem with Jack, since his hearing was, if anything, even worse than his eyesight. My hearing, on the other hand, was almost supernatural. If you want to be a good liar, job one is being a good listener.

I couldn't take a chance that Ed might still recognize me from our close encounter at the crash site, so I walked down the block and back up the alley to the Dumpster out back of the Mason Jar. By going to the last booth, Ed and his boys had made the mistake of sitting next to the old screen door that goes out to the alley. Crouched next to the Dumpster, I could hear every word they said, even if I couldn't see who was saying what. It didn't really matter. The smell was epically ripe, however, so there was a battle being fought between my nose and ears while I listened in.

Unidentified male voice number one said, "I still don't understand how a probe could crash a year before it was even launched." Neither did I, but Bobby Ray did, and that put our team two steps ahead of Ed Hemet's. Or so I thought, until unidentified male voice number two started to unwind an explanation so full of complicated words that it made Bobby Ray's version sound like a kindergarten lesson. In fact the only words I recognized were when they all took a break to order their food. This voice made "chicken salad sandwich" sound like boring technical mumbo jumbo. It made me appreciate Bobby Ray's skill at dumbing it down for me.

As if I needed further proof that these guys were from out of state, nobody ordered anything fried. The fryer at the Mason Jar takes up the better part of the kitchen. No local would leave there without greasy fingers to show for the experience. When the waitress was out of earshot, I heard them get back to business.

"What are the chances that the disc dislodged as it was going through reentry?" the first voice asked.

"Statistically?" the boring guy asked.

"Something that kid said . . ." A new voice joined in, Ed Hemet's voice. I accidentally pressed my knee into an old Coke bottle as I leaned in to hear better. If they'd still put Coke in glass bottles, it wouldn't have made such a sickeningly loud crunch. I held my breath, expecting a half dozen men to burst out through the screen door, guns drawn.

They didn't. I got lucky, because at the same time that I'd made my little mistake, the waitress had made a bigger one by dropping a tray full of salad plates on her way from the kitchen. I think the fact that nobody'd ordered any fried staples had thrown her off her game. When the commotion died down, Ed continued, "That weird chunky kid said NASA. *NASA*. Just out of nowhere. Odd."

The description of Bobby Ray was cruel, but hard to argue with. As much as I'd hoped Ed Hemet had given up on us, he had not. I felt the need to put some distance between me and them at that instant. That's when the screen door swung open with a spring-stretching sound that made my heart jump into my neck.

It was the waitress, with a dustpan full of glass and lettuce. Her name was Ethel. She'd worked at the Mason Jar my whole life. I figured with a name like Ethel she had probably shot out of her momma wearing a little apron and holding an order pad. I knew her, but she didn't really know me, since my parents weren't exactly regulars at the Mason Jar.

"What kind of trouble are you getting into back here, kid?" Ethel the waitress said to me in a voice that had obviously been calibrated to be heard by the practically deaf One-Eyed Jack. I knew shushing her would only make matters worse, so I had no choice but to spin a lie that was breathtaking in its complexity. It involved collecting bottles to raise money for a charity helping the victims of the recent Eurasian typhoon. Even the typhoon was fiction. But whatever I was selling, Ethel was buying.

It was all good. Until the door spring stretched again.

"We're in a little hurry here," Ed Hemet said in a

not altogether hurried way to Ethel. He saw me.

"The Boy Scout," he said. I turned as though there might be somebody going for a merit badge behind me, but then I remembered that was what I'd told him that day at the crash site. It's always troubling when someone remembers your lies better than you do.

We had covered the whole fight-or-flight instinct in science class the previous winter. When the cornered animal is a liar, there is a third option. Next thing I knew, I was sitting in a chair next to the booth, while these guys alternated between giving me the third degree and eating their healthy-as-you-can-get-in-the-Mason-Jar lunches.

First thing I did was admit that the Boy Scout story wasn't true. It's important when you're spinning a new web of lies to make sure you clear out the old one first. The know-it-all guy tried to trip me up. I told them that I had seen the crashed probe. That it had nearly crashed into me, in fact. The know-it-all seemed to forget about the missing disc and started asking me about angle of descent and other stuff Bobby Ray would have appreciated about a million times more than me. I demonstrated the crash with the pepper shaker and got the whole table sneezing on impact. Ed kept trying to bring up—without actually saying so—the disc. But I got off that real quick to describe sounds that the probe had made as it was cooling down in the dirt. Even though it was all made up based on the cycles of Momma's dishwasher, even Mr. Know-It-All believed me, right down to the final release of steam.

"Moisture must have seeped in though the thermal seals." He nodded to my dishwasher description.

The rest of the table was ready to buy me a cookie and send me on my way, but Ed Hemet looked at me like he was Superman x-raying my brain. He could break me if he got me alone. I knew it and he knew it.

He didn't get a chance. As if it were a sign from above, the base shuttle van pulled up at its stop. I told the government crew that I had to be on that shuttle to go to the base to visit my big shot uncle. I said he had lots of pull in Washington, D.C. I suspected that Ed knew full well I was making everything up. But he let me go anyway.

I ran for it. Even though I wasn't technically allowed to ride without Justine, the driver seemed to recognize me from before and let me on. Before I had time to really think things through, I was heading for Justine's yellow house.

Chapter NINETEEN

Unfortunately, it wasn't as easy to get past the guard at the base as it was to get past the driver of the van. He made me get out and wait while he called Justine's place. So much for surprising her.

Justine came to claim me with some young Korean woman. I found out that this was her momma. It was straightaway clear where Justine got her exotic good looks. No wonder she was so set apart from the other Kudzu girls. Justine didn't seem happy to see me. My heart hit the dirt; I couldn't chalk this up to Momma's Cheat Loaf. Even her momma seemed down. I wondered what Justine had told her about me.

But as we walked back to their yellow building,

Justine explained that her daddy had gotten his orders that morning. I wasn't really familiar with all the military terminology, but it was pretty clear that it wasn't a good thing as far as Justine was concerned. I was going to tell her about my interrogation at the Mason Jar, but it didn't seem like a good time.

"One year," her momma said. She spoke English fine, but she still had a pretty heavy accent. Of course, from my perspective my momma and daddy had accents too. Pretty much anyone not born in Kudzu sounded funny to me.

I wasn't sure if she was saying one year like that wasn't so long, or like it was forever. I know it felt like forever to Justine. Next time she saw her daddy, she'd be thirteen. That's a big difference.

Their house was neat but plain. No library there. Obviously they couldn't collect a lot of junk, since they had to move around so much. I felt awkward, like I'd interrupted something. There was a pile of balled-up Kleenex on the kitchen table.

Justine's momma busied herself tidying up, even

though I said not to bother on my account. Besides, other than the spent Kleenex, the place was neat as a pin. Even sad, she looked so much younger than my momma.

Trying to think of something to say, I asked Justine if she could speak any Korean. She said that she was born there. That amazed me. Then she said some of the words her momma taught her. I'm not sure if you would call Korean a romance language, but it sounded close enough for me. But as much as I would have liked to heed some of Tommy Doolittle's advice, I didn't think Justine was in the mood for love's savage spectacle.

Justine's momma was starting to cry, even while she was Swiffering the floor. Justine must have seen it coming too, because she grabbed my hand and said that we could go to the PX to buy more Kleenex. As much as I felt awkward about the whole situation, the idea of finally getting to go inside the PX for a moment took me back to a happier time when all I'd cared about was cheap chocolate.

The inside of the PX was kind of disappointing. It

looked like they'd pretty much took a Wal-Mart and shrunk it. The Hershey bars were a little cheaper, but way more than twenty-five cents. Whoever had told me that was a stinking liar. And not in a good way, like my way.

Justine bought a box of Kleenex and some frozen dinners. I picked up a giant Hershey bar anyway, just because it seemed a shame to have gone all that way and not get one.

"I don't think my mother will feel much like cooking tonight," Justine said. I wondered if, being from Korea and all, her momma made weirder dishes than mine. I thought it would be interesting to get them together and see, when Justine's momma was feeling better. Then I wondered if she'd be crying for a year, and that depressed me. Maybe selfishly, because Justine's sad momma would surely have a negative impact on my wooing of Justine.

When we were waiting to check out, I noticed that the lady in front of us was the shuttle-van-riding army bride. She smiled at the cashier and seemed to be doing okay. Not great maybe, but okay. That made me feel better for Justine's momma somehow. And that made me feel better for me.

When we got back to Justine's place, her momma was surrounded by a half dozen other women from the base. Someone had made coffee and brought over a bag of store-bought cookies. One of the ladies was holding Justine's momma's hand. I got the feeling that this was a routine event on the base, looking at how relaxed some of them were. I suddenly felt like it was no place for a twelve-year-old boy.

Sometimes I lie for fun. Sometimes to get myself out of a fix. But sometimes I lie to make somebody else feel better about something.

"I know your daddy will come home fine," I said. I'm not sure it worked.

I got on the van and went home, thinking about what I could do to help Justine.

When I got home, Momma yelled out from the kitchen that Bobby Ray had come looking for me earlier. Somehow, I knew he'd be back. This day was not getting any better. Clearly he was under the impression that we were friends now. Maybe that would be okay over the summer, but when school started up, I could not be seen in the company of a science-loving, hand-washing, plate-tapping freak. Besides, I had to devote the rest of the summer to cheering up Justine and keeping her mind off worrisome thoughts.

I plopped down on the sofa, confused and hopeless. Then I noticed Momma had left her child psychology book on the side table. There were two bookmarks in it. I opened to the first, a chapter called "Compulsive Lying." I took that bookmark out and went to the second marked chapter. It was titled, "Pediatric Obsessive-Compulsive Disorder." That one I read.

It described kids who were obsessed with one particular subject. Kids who washed their hands until they were chapped and red. Kids who had strange habits and tics. It described Bobby Ray Dobbs.

I read the whole chapter, and even though it was loaded with words I'd never come across before, when I'd finished it, I had an idea to kill two birds with one rock. Justine and I were going to cure Bobby Ray.

Chapter **TWENTY**

Next morning I got up and read the next day's paper, as was my new habit. This one actually had kind of an interesting story about a Georgia man who found a ten-foot-long one-thousand-pound wild pig. They named the pig "Hogstro," which I guess was because of Monstro, the whale that eats Pinocchio. Pinocchio was another story that I never much cared for. I thought it presented an unrealistic take on the consequences of lying.

Anyway, this man in Georgia said he'd gotten a picture of Hogstro before it disappeared into the woods. The paper printed the picture, but the account below it featured some killjoy experts asking if the whole thing was just a tall tale. They even showed how the picture could have been faked with a fifteen-dollar computer program. Obviously the reporters of the *New York Times* didn't know how to enjoy a good story. I could teach them a thing or two.

I called Justine and told her about my plan to cure Bobby Ray. She seemed doubtful at first, but I convinced her that if we didn't do it, nobody would.

Momma picked Justine up and dropped us both off in Shady Brook. I briefed Justine as we walked over to Bobby Ray's house. I told her that the book suggested a lot of strategies, but the one that I understood was called "exposure and ritual prevention therapy." This involved, in Bobby Ray's case, getting him good and dirty, while hiding his wetnaps.

When Bobby Ray came to the door, he seemed happy to see us. *If only he knew*, I thought. *If only he knew.*

"I went by the crash site with a metal detector, and I think Ed Hemet's guys might have missed something," I said. Now, I didn't actually own a metal detector, but Bobby Ray didn't know that, and he went running for his shoes.

On the way to the woods, I initiated phase two,

inspired by Justine's misadventure with my Little Debbie Double Chocolate Swiss Cake Roll. We could laugh about her misfortune now, but Bobby Ray wouldn't be laughing about his. The goal was to rid Bobby Ray of his wetnaps. I thought about having Justine distract him while I slipped them out of his pocket, but I'm a liar, not a pickpocket. If he caught me, the whole rest of the plan could be blown. This called for a subtler approach.

I opened the giant Hershey bar I'd bought at the PX and split it into thirds. It was half-melted from being in my pocket, so it was a mess already. Bobby Ray, of course, wanted the end with the wrapper still on it. But just before I handed it to him, I slipped off the wrapper and gave him the hunk of soft, naked Hershey bar. I pulled this move off with a magician's sleight of hand, so Bobby Ray didn't even realize he was grabbing melty chocolate until it was squishing between his fingers. He looked like he was going to die right there. He shoved the whole piece into his mouth and dug deep for one of his wetnaps.

Justine and I finished our chunks, and showed Bobby Ray our brown hands. He looked repulsed. Then I caught him completely by surprise.

"Say, Bobby Ray," I said in a casual way that suggested that this hadn't all been rehearsed, "you think you could give Justine and me some of them wetnaps in your pocket?" He looked at me like I had just asked him to give me one of his kidneys.

"Liar gave you some of his Hershey bar," Justine reminded him, like he could have forgotten, looking at our disgusting hands.

"Yeah, fair's fair," I added.

Reluctantly and slowly Bobby Ray pulled two wetnaps out of his pocket. He fished around and realized that they were his *last* two.

"Here, you can share," he said as he handed one to Justine and quickly pocketed the other.

"We can't share, Bobby Ray," Justine said.

"Do you know how many germs can live on a used wetnap?" I said. I had no idea, of course, but clearly Bobby Ray did. This was his language I was speaking, and I could not be denied. With heavy sorrow he pulled out his last wetnap and offered it to me. I think he was reevaluating the whole cost of friendship during the moment that he held it out there.

"Thanks!" I said brightly as I grabbed it away and ripped it open. When Justine and I tossed the drying wetnaps into a Dumpster behind the beauty parlor, I think a little piece of Bobby Ray went with them.

So we entered the woods with Bobby Ray defenseless. Finding the fresh dirt where the crash had been covered up, I pointed at a spot and said, "There." I knelt in the dirt and started digging with my bare hands. Bobby Ray watched with his jaw dropped, like he was watching man land on the moon. He looked over to Justine. She shrugged and dropped to her knees to join the dig.

"You didn't bring a shovel?" Bobby Ray asked with a wobbly voice.

"It's not like I planned all this," I said. At that moment I pulled out a piece of wire that I had planted in there earlier. I acted like it was a fishing line with a record-breaking largemouth bass on the other end. Justine helped me pretend to pull at it.

Schooley/McCorkle

"Whatever's at the other end, it's something big," she said.

I could see Bobby Ray was in conflict between his obsessions and his compulsions. Just like I'd planned it.

"Come on down here, Bobby Ray. Give us a hand," I yelled.

"Yeah, you can dig too, you know," Justine added.

He did it. Right there, dropped down and began to claw at the earth. We stopped to watch for a second, it was such an amazing sight to see dirt getting under the smooth-cut nails of Bobby Ray Dobbs. It may have been a first. Dirt flew as he backhoed away following that wire down.

It's really a shame that the wire was just tied around an old horseshoe. When he pulled up at that line and the shoe twirled on the end, it was a lot like a bass master catching an old boot, I guess. Justine struggled to keep a straight face, since she knew who put that horseshoe there. It was nice to see her happy, even if it was at Bobby Ray's expense. Still, it was for his own good; he just wouldn't know that for a while.

His eyes wetted up a little as he looked at his dirt-caked hands and realized that he had no means to wash them clean.

"Do you think Ed Hemet did that to make us look stupid if we ever told anyone about the crash?" I hypothesized. Bobby Ray suddenly looked less angry, like he hadn't thought of that. Then he just broke away from us and started running toward home.

I called after him, "We're doing this to save you, Bobby Ray. This is for your own good!" He just kept going.

We kept up pretty good behind him, since he wasn't what you would call a marathoner. When he dashed into his house, no doubt to his little sink by the stairs, he had one more surprise. Unlike in the older parts of town, the modern homes of Shady Brook had big knobs right by the front door, where someone could easily shut off the water to the whole house, in case of an emergency, like a burst pipe or an exploding toilet. Bobby Ray got to that sink, but one little pathetic drip was all he got. His momma would probably call a plumber who would charge her fifty bucks to turn a knob. But we figured it was cheaper than therapy for Bobby Ray, so a worthy expense.

As Justine and me headed home, we could hear Bobby Ray's sad wail. Our work was finished for the day; we'd done enough.

Chapter **TWENTY-ONE**

We didn't see Bobby Ray for a long time after the day of the dirt. I went over to his house a few times, but his momma always came to the door and looked at me as though I were the one who'd shut off her water supply. Which, of course, I was, but she didn't have proof of that, and I felt like "innocent until proven guilty" should apply.

While she was trying to get rid of me, I'd hear Bobby Ray shout down the stairs, "Tell him I'm not home."

Bobby Ray was not a natural-born liar by any stretch.

I talked with Justine about the events of that day many times over the next few weeks. We agreed that we'd rushed his program a little, given that the book suggested a six-month period for the exposure and ritual prevention therapy. But we weren't giving up, just giving Bobby Ray a chance to recover.

In the meantime we kicked around together enough to be unofficial best friends. Momma and Daddy came to like her pretty strongly too, I think, based on how they acted around her. At least they stopped looking for trouble in their books and let everything flow without comment. She came over for my momma's weird cooking, and I went over for her momma's. Not that there was an actual competition, but I think her momma won the question of which was weirdest. Could be just because I was used to my momma's, but I knew she would never serve up thin slices of raw beef. Or any beef for that matter. Justine's momma did something she called barbecue, but it was nothing like the goods from Mr. Black's Rib Shack. It was kind of tasty, though, once you got past the initial shock of all that garlic.

I helped Justine write letters to her daddy, doing what I could to make life in Kudzu sound fun so he wouldn't worry. I'm not sure he believed the story about the circus monkeys, but hopefully he got a grin out of it.

Ed Hemet never did show up again. In a week or two we almost forgot about him. I did continue to read the next day's papers, though, mainly to figure out if there was any truth to the Hogstro story, which somehow became an issue in the presidential campaign. One of the candidates aligned himself with people who believed in Hogstro. I'm not sure why, but it did get him a five-point rise in the polls.

Justine continued to visit C. C. Lee until he really couldn't remember her name anymore. Soon enough, his family came in from all over to be with him. I knew he didn't have many days left, but by that time they knew it too.

Soon enough, school was less than a week away, and even though the summer had been the best ever, thanks to Justine, I felt like I had unfinished business. Assuming he didn't opt out for homeschooling now, Bobby Ray was going to be a mess if I didn't do something. And, of course, there was the matter of kissing Justine. But I knew that would happen eventually, when the conditions were right. I'd given up on the *Oprah* plan, so I'd just have to make my own big heart somehow.

Then the rain came.

Just like the paper said it would, it poured buckets for a week. I hardly saw Justine, because it was so hard to get around, with accidents and mud everywhere. At least I knew the day the sun would come out. I actually bet Daddy. Maybe I should have bet somebody on Hogstro, since by then I had read that it was indeed a big fat lie. Interestingly, the revelation didn't seem to hurt the candidate who'd staked his campaign on a mythical thousand-pound wild pig. Like I always said, people like a good story if it's more interesting than the truth.

Knowing that the hot August sun would reappear on this particular day, I was ready to collect my winnings and soak up my last hours of freedom before school started. When I got up, it was still drizzling a little, which Daddy pointed out as he got ready for work. But I knew clear and breezy skies, and five bucks for me, were coming.

Before I headed over to Justine's, I checked the next day's news, just out of habit. My peek into the future didn't have many days left, and then the disc would have nothing but history on it. I read over the latest poll results, wishing that the disc went through November, because the results of the election would be big news to know. This was the same story I'd read, I realized, way back when we'd first skimmed through the pages. The day we'd found out about C. C. Lee, and I'd discovered it was looking grim for Momma and Daddy's pick from New York, mainly because he was on the wrong side of the Hogstro issue.

That's when I saw it.

It wasn't really a huge story in proportion to the others on that page, but the headline was this:

DEATH TOLL UNKNOWN IN SOUTHERN RAIL DISASTER

It was the part after that headline that made my head pound and my hands shake. From my current

event report experience I knew that the part after
the headline was called a dateline. It tells people
where the story that they are about to read happened.
The dateline for this train disaster story:

KUDZU

Chapter **TWENTY-TWO**

I'd gotten used to knowing what would happen the next day, but I'd also gotten used to knowing that it wouldn't matter one way or another to my life. But this changed everything. I couldn't even read the whole story, since most of it was continued on an inside page that wasn't on the disc. But what I could read was enough to know we were in horrible trouble:

A massive train derailment resulted in widespread death and destruction when a toxic cloud of chlorine gas was leaked into the atmosphere of the small town of Kudzu. Eyewitness accounts say that at approximately 11:20 yesterday morning the westbound locomotive struck an automobile on the track

near the town's center. At least two tankers holding
the highly volatile gas split open and released . . .

Continued on page A19.

I read and reread that paragraph. But I wasn't
exactly thinking straight, because it was a few minutes before I realized that the "11:20 yesterday
morning" in the article was 11:20 *this morning* to me.
My eyes darted to the clock at the bottom of the
screen—10:32. Over the course of the summer I had
been sleeping later and later. I'd sworn that I'd get up
earlier today to get back in the habit for school. If I
had, I would have had a lot more time to do something smart right then.

I could call the police, but I knew that my reputation would, at best, slow their response. There was no
time for twenty questions and certainly no time to
tell the whole unlikely story of the Vespucci probe.
Even in thinking about it, I couldn't figure out how to
tell it like the truth.

Calling Ed Hemet was another possibility. He'd
believe me about the probe, but he was probably in

Washington, D.C., and by the time they reacted up there, we'd all be in a toxic cloud down here.

Even the most extreme option, telling Momma and Daddy, wasn't possible. Daddy was at the college, and he always turned off his cell phone when he was with a class. Momma was out picking up pie supplies, and besides, she refused to even carry a cell phone. Something about the dangers of electromagnetic radiation, which, compared to a killer cloud, suddenly didn't seem so bad.

It was up to me and me alone to save Kudzu.

I called Justine. The base was east of town, and the tracks ran right alongside it. If she could figure out a way to get the train to slow down, I could get to the intersection and make sure no cars went through.

But once I had Justine all good and worked up, I had a terrible thought.

"If it's in tomorrow's paper, we can't stop it; we're helpless," I said.

"I once heard somebody on TV say something like 'The future is not written, but ours to write,'" she said.

"I'm pretty sure that guy didn't have a subscription to tomorrow's *New York Times*," I said. "Maybe we should just get everyone we can far away from the tracks and hope for the best." But then I thought of Momma downtown, loading up her backseat with pie tins.

"There's only one way to find out if we can change the future," Justine said, and I knew she was right. We had a destiny to fulfill. I hoped. Because, otherwise, we were on a suicide mission.

I told Justine to make a big sign that said STOP and hang it by the tracks by the base. Meanwhile I would go to the crossing and wave down the cars. Drivers were always trying to beat the train across those tracks. Somebody's luck was due to run out today, unless I could stop them.

I threw on my clothes and ran out of the house, hoping Justine could make my job unnecessary. Then again, I wasn't sure what she could do to actually stop a freight train, but she could be powerfully persuasive when she set her mind to it. And she didn't have a lying reputation to live down.

It was 10:45, and I didn't have time for a leisurely

stroll downtown. I pulled out my old two-wheeler, which I hadn't been on all summer, and took off like a bat out of you know where. Shortcuts were out of the question because it was still spitting rain and the ground was swampy and spongy. My tires sunk in deep the minute I pulled off the road.

Pumping the pedals until my legs ached, I flew past the entrance to Shady Brook. It was then that I sparked on a hard fact: I might be able to get the cars on one side of the tracks to stop, but I couldn't be on both sides. I turned around.

I pounded on Bobby Ray's front door and threw rocks at his bedroom window. His Momma was obviously not home, or she'd have been calling 9-1-1. I heard his voice call down, "I'm not home."

He's a genius and all, but how stupid did he think I was? "Bobby Ray, it's an emergency. I need your help!" I screamed.

He opened the front door and said, "You better not be lying, Liar."

I told Bobby Ray to grab his bike and follow me. He made a funny face.

"What?" I asked.

"I don't have a bike," he said.

"You have a computer in your bedroom!" I screamed. "How can you not have a bicycle?"

"I know how to *work* a computer," Bobby Ray said, and shrugged.

"You mean you . . . You never learned how to ride a two-wheeler?" I said, not quite believing it. By the look on his face, I'd say it was doubtful if he'd even conquered a Big Wheel.

Bobby Ray rode on the seat behind me, which slowed me down, but I had no choice. He was the only other person that could get this story in the short strokes. He started to think out loud. "If the train left the chemical plant in Dixon City at ten and was going sixty miles an hour, that would put it at the army base in about five minutes from now," he said.

"This isn't a word problem, Bobby Ray," I said. "This is a real problem."

"That would mean that the train would pass through town by eleven, ordinarily," Bobby Ray continued, pretty much ignoring me. I thought about it, and that actually sounded about right.

"Maybe it's running late," I said, ridiculously out of breath.

"Or maybe Justine gets it to stop, and then it gets going again," he said.

Justine really had gotten the train to stop, at least temporarily. She hadn't painted a big sign, though. An anonymous tip to the base police that the train conductor was number five on the FBI's Most Wanted list had done the trick. Justine had obviously learned from the master, but I knew she would only use her powers for good.

The base police radioed ahead and flagged down the train as it came past the base. When they'd boarded it, it was hard to tell who was more annoyed, the innocent conductor or the police. They let the train go after a ten-minute background check on the conductor. What they didn't know was that the train then had an extra passenger aboard.

Schooley/McCorkle

Chapter TWENTY-THREE

I didn't know Justine was on board the train at that point, which was probably just as well. If I'd had any more adrenaline shooting through me at that moment, I might have just exploded. Bobby Ray and me got to the crossing about five minutes before the accident was supposed to happen. How I was going to get the cars to heed the flashing lights became a trickier task when I noticed that the signal was lying down flat on the road. Judging from the tire tracks in the mud, someone must have come along and skidded into it sometime in the wee hours. We didn't exactly have a giant police force—it was two part-timers and an old lady who worked the phone—so it was clear no one had even noticed the downed signal yet. It was probably hard to tell in the rain. I tried to lift it up, but it weighed a ton and was half-sunk in mud. I knew better than to ask Bobby Ray for a hand. Fool me once, and all that.

The only option was for the two of us to stand in the middle of the road in the rain and wave our arms like idiots.

Momma's car was the first one to come to a stop in front of me. She looked through her intermittent wipers for a minute like she couldn't believe her only son was standing in the road in the rain and waving his arms like an idiot. I could barely believe it myself. It was a good thing that I had that downed signal to point to, because it was a lot easier to tell her I'd seen that and known the train was coming soon than to get into the whole *New York Times*-warp story.

As the laws of chance would have it, the first car that Bobby Ray stopped was his momma's. Unfortunately, he couldn't help but reach for the longer explanation. I could just make out his momma's voice saying, "I just knew I'd rue the day I let you near that Liar boy." I think she said it loud on purpose, for my benefit.

At the same time, in the engineer's compartment, Justine was begging for him to stop the train before he got to Kudzu. But it was a noisy place to be, and the story she was telling sounded crazy. Wormhole? Come on.

"I'M ALREADY BEHIND SCHEDULE THANKS TO THAT MORON WHO CALLED THE POLICE ON ME," he said in his onboard voice.

"I'M THAT MORON!" Justine screamed back. This proved—as if I ever needed proof—that honesty isn't always the best policy. In fact, sometimes it's the worst policy. Like when you're trying to get someone to stop a freight train.

Bobby Ray and I were feeling pretty triumphant. After all, with family holding the line, even with the car horns honking, nobody was getting through until after the train had passed safely. We were going to pull it off and change the future.

Cool.

Then a big SUV decided to pass and cross in the

wrong lane. I ran to head him off. It was Ed Hemet. He looked at me from behind green sunglasses, which was stupid, since it had just stopped raining. The sun would be breaking through soon, but it was hardly sunglass weather yet. For a second I thought of the five dollars Daddy would owe me, and I hoped I would be alive to collect.

"I'm a liar," I shouted to Ed and the world, "but this is the whole honest truth. I found the CD off the Vespucci probe, and it made me be able to see into the future. And I'm trying to stop the train from crashing and killing all of us."

It felt good to get that off my chest.

Ed Hemet squinted at me, his face creased and cold. I thought he might be calculating how much prison time a twelve-year-old could rack up.

What happened next was pretty amazing. Just on my word Ed Hemet pulled his SUV across the other lane. Then he waved the base shuttle van out of line and ordered the driver to do the same on the other side. I never thought Ed Hemet would make me feel safe and secure, but for that moment he did.

I could hear the train whistle in the distance.

It was Justine on board pulling the cord, and she was not messing around. The engineer wasn't exactly pleased, but he let her do that much since at least it wouldn't slow him down. He'd turn her over to the authorities when he got to his next stop, he told her.

For once the sad sound made me feel good. Then the crash happened.

It wasn't the train, yet. It was up ahead on the tracks. The saturated ground beneath a stack of kudzu-covered junked cars at the scrap yard gave way. The cars spilled over with a sound that might as well have been a train crash, as harsh and earth-shaking as it was. It was as though it were happening in slow motion. We watched the top car turn over and over, metal creaking, until it finally came to a stop.

On the tracks.

I flashed onto the story again in my mind. It said that the train hit an automobile on the tracks. It didn't say that the car was an old kudzu-covered junker. Then again, it didn't say that it *wasn't*.

The kudzu was the real problem. With that old

heap covered in green, once it came to a stop, it was as if it were purposely camouflaged to fade into the background. There was no way the engineer would be able to see that.

The tracks started to vibrate. The train came around the bend. In moments there would be impact.

On board, Justine was arguing with the engineer, so he didn't see Ed Hemet and our mommas waving their arms like idiots as the train approached.

I've always functioned best under pressure. But this was a new level. The sun was starting to stab through the clouds, but Daddy's five dollars was the furthest thing from my mind. What I did notice was Momma's backseat, full of shiny foil pie tins. Like the hand of my maker was guiding me, I dove in and grabbed an armful.

The train was almost on top of us when I hurled those pie tins down toward the kudzu-covered car. Momma had once said that the word "Frisbee" came from the brand name stamped on a pie tin. Kids used to like to throw them for fun, until someone had the bright idea of making them out of plastic. This wasn't for fun, but the effect was the same. Those tins soared in the air, just in front of the train. Ed joined me. And Bobby Ray did too.

The sun finally broke through, and it hit those floating shiny plates full force. Justine pointed, and the engineer turned to see the strange sight. A hundred UFOs reflected sunlight against his window like a disco ball. Then he saw them bounce off of something growing out of the middle of the track. When he reached for the brake, he felt Justine's hand on his, helping to pull like her life depended on it. All of our lives depended on it, really.

Sparks and grease and mud flew all over us as the train screamed to a hard stop. The noise was amazing. When the train finally made contact with that car, it was with just a light tap, as if the kudzu itself was the final cushion against disaster.

For a minute everyone was just clam quiet. They were all counting their blessings, but I was holding my breath, hoping that there wasn't yet another surprise like the falling kudzu car.

It never came. Justine came bounding out of that

engine with a mile-wide smile. If we had been in a movie, I would have kissed her full on the lips right there. But we were surrounded by people, so we made do with a high five. I looked over to see Bobby Ray, covered in mud and grease, and yet laughing. Maybe this was all just part of his cure.

Chapter TWENTY-FOUR

The next day we all went to the college to look at the *New York Times*. On the way there Bobby Ray talked Daddy's ear off, all about the physics of stopping trains and why we hadn't all died, mathematically speaking. I'm not sure if Daddy credited me with this sudden burst of genius or realized that I'd pulled another good one over on him, but he was speechless either way.

We walked up the big steps and went to find that day's paper. Most of the front page looked exactly like the one I had seen the day before. But there in the corner, where the end of Kudzu had been foretold, was instead a follow-up on the fellow who'd made up the story of Hogstro. Apparently he was being offered a job in the new administration if the pro-Hogstro candidate should win. There was one other new article too. It told of a railway close call in a small town in the South.

We made a deal with Ed Hemet that we'd give up the disc and never talk about it to anyone; in return he wouldn't charge us with stealing government property. I'm not sure he was actually serious about sending us up the river, but I flashed on Tommy Doolittle's tale of tragic romance and decided not to take any chances. We needed a cover story. I volunteered for that job. When the reporter from the *New York Times* called, it was all I could do to not tell her the role her very own paper played, but I had promised Ed.

The whopper that came out of my talk with that reporter was some of my best work. It told of three kids who'd had a simultaneous mysterious vision and had foreseen the train disaster. Working independently, they'd all run from their houses to the tracks and done everything they could to stop the accident from happening. Stephen King would have been proud.

Someone up in Chicago must have read that article, or one of the hundreds of others that were written after it. By the time poor C. C. Lee met his reward, Justine, Bobby Ray, and me were the most famous people in Kudzu. When Oprah's people called the house, Momma thought it was a crank, but I knew it was real. It was like I'd wished it to happen and now it was.

School started, but we weren't there. We were all on a plane to Chicago as Oprah's special guests. On the way I convinced Bobby Ray and Justine to let me tell the lying parts; they could fill in the parts that had actually happened. It wasn't like we wanted to lie. Ed Hemet *insisted* on it. This was Government Approved.

Our mommas went with us, since my daddy had to start the new semester and Bobby Ray's daddy was on one of his never-ending business trips. Of course, Justine's father was still overseas at some kind of secure undisclosed location.

Oprah's people picked us up at the airport in a giant limo and took us to the most deluxe hotel I'd ever seen. Then again, it's not like there are any four-star lodgings in Dixon County, or in our whole state, for that matter. These Chicago rooms were huge and spotless, which pleased Bobby Ray to no end. Ever since the train incident he had been backing off the extremes of his problem, but the road to wellness still stretched a ways before him.

When the time came to meet Oprah, I thought Bobby Ray would have a stroke. I was feeling a little queasy myself. The production people told us a bunch of stuff that we would never remember when the time came.

"Look at Oprah, not the camera," a nice lady told us just before they said we were on. The light on the camera came on, and we all stared at it. But then Oprah started talking in that famous way she talks, and it was like we were just hangin' with her like she was a normal person. I told my part of the story, throwing in new details I'd cooked up for the national audience. I said I had a model train that kept going off the tracks at 11:20 each day for a week, and so did Bobby Ray and Justine. Bobby Ray started to speak, but

Justine elbowed him good in the ribs. I don't think the camera caught it, though. Then I said that I had seen a ghost cloud descending over the HO-gauge tracks.

"The chlorine gas," Oprah explained helpfully.

"Must have been," I said, and nodded.

Then I described how I'd heard screams and horrible grinding metal in my dreams. Oprah squeezed my hand. I looked at her sorrowfully, imitating a kid who had been haunted by disturbing psychic visions.

"I knew it was going to happen, Oprah, and I couldn't let it. I just couldn't let it." I choked up to a swell of audience applause. Oprah turned to Bobby Ray.

"What about you, Bobby Ray?" Oprah asked him.

I jumped in, suddenly composed. "Same deal," I told her. "Justine, too, same exact deal." I think Oprah was getting peeved at me, though again, I don't think the camera caught it. I did let them talk about pulling on the brake and throwing the pie tins. I didn't want to be a camera hog, after all.

Oprah talked to us some more during the commercial, but it was stuff I don't think she really cared about, like what grade we were in and where exactly Kudzu was. When the commercial break ended and the camera light came back on, Oprah smiled and said she had a surprise for one of her "psychic heroes," which is what she had taken to calling us. Our hotel rooms had big plasma screen TVs, but Oprah had a bigger one. It lowered down from above us, and Oprah said she had a special guest coming to us via satellite from a secret location.

Justine's daddy was on that TV.

"I'm proud of you, baby," he told her. I was afraid Justine was just going to lose it right there and start spilling the truth all over Oprah. Oprah looked like she was ready to let loose the waterworks herself. But Justine was tough, and that's what I loved about her. She sniffled a little and told her daddy she loved him, but she didn't take down the team or compromise the mission. Her daddy would have been *really* proud of that, I thought.

That fast, it was over. We weren't on for the whole

show, but I did get to meet the Hogstro liar on his way out for his segment. We passed in the hall and I shook his hand, a moment shared between two world-class storytellers.

Oprah, being Oprah, let us have the limo for the rest of the day and gave us gift certificates to the fancy stores on Michigan Avenue. But there was only one place I wanted to go.

"Museum of Science and Industry," I told the driver, like I was used to telling drivers where to take me. We ditched Bobby Ray at the Apollo 8 module, and I grabbed Justine by the hand and ran to the body science hall.

BUH-BUMP.

We were getting close. I could follow that sound of a simulated heartbeat.

BUH-BUMP.

It was huge, that giant heart. Red and blue light flashed up the sides to show how blood flowed in and out. Hidden speakers pounded out that rhythm that you could feel in your teeth.

BUH-BUMP.

I grabbed Justine and led her into the left ventricle.

We climbed some steps, and soon we were in the heart of the heart. That fake heartbeat was deafening in there.

BUH-BUMP. BUH-BUMP. BUH-BUMP.

My heart was going like a hummingbird compared to it. We were standing under red lights, so even if one of us blushed, the other wouldn't know.

BUH-BUMP.

Justine must have thought I was acting crazy, and I guess I was. All summer long this had been the future I'd been looking forward to most. And now it was real and here. Yet it felt weirdly unreal now that it was actually happening. I grabbed both her hands and let a group of kindergartners stampede past until we were alone again.

BUH-BUMP.

"There's something I've wanted to do since the first day you walked into Faulkner Middle School," I said. She looked at me funny as I built up the nerve to do it. I could hear in the distance another herd of kindergartners climbing into the aorta. Soon they too would be in this chamber. I took a deep breath. I think

I even quivered in anticipation. It was now or never—

Then she kissed me.

I didn't see that coming.

No lie.

BOB SCHOOLEY and **MARK McCORKLE** are feature film writers who created the hit animated series **KIM POSSIBLE**, which airs on the Disney Channel. This is their first novel. They both live in Los Angeles.